"I'm not quite sure why I insisted that Cassie and her mother—and that darned dog of hers—be in-house babysitters for Sadie. It was kind of like adjusting a race strategy on the fly at Talladega after a big crash. I threw out the charts and went with my gut."
—Ethan Hunt

"I was a marine. I've fought enemies of all sorts. But I can't fight what I'm starting to feel for Sadie… and her dad."
—Cassie Conners

"People only kiss the way I saw Daddy and Cassie kiss when they're really in love…I think."
—Sadie Hunt

"I know my trips to Mexico have interfered with our team, with my driving. Our crew chief isn't to blame for my mistakes, no matter what he says."
—Trey Sanford

MARISA CARROLL

is the pen name of sisters Carol Wagner and Marian Franz. The team has been writing bestselling books for almost twenty-five years. During that time they have published more than forty titles, most for the Harlequin Superromance line, and are the recipients of several industry awards, including a Lifetime Achievement Award from *Romantic Times BOOKreviews* and a RITA® Award nomination from Romance Writers of America. Their books have been featured on the *USA TODAY,* Waldenbooks and B. Dalton bestseller lists. The sisters live near each other in northwestern Ohio, surrounded by children, grandchildren, brothers, sisters, aunts, uncles, cousins and old and dear friends.

//////NASCAR®

NO HOLDS BARRED

Marisa Carroll

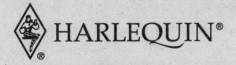

HARLEQUIN®

TORONTO • NEW YORK • LONDON
AMSTERDAM • PARIS • SYDNEY • HAMBURG
STOCKHOLM • ATHENS • TOKYO • MILAN • MADRID
PRAGUE • WARSAW • BUDAPEST • AUCKLAND

Recycling programs
for this product may
not exist in your area.

ISBN-13: 978-0-373-18524-5

NO HOLDS BARRED

Copyright © 2009 by Harlequin Books S.A.

Carol I. Wagner and Marian L. Franz are acknowledged
as the authors of this work.

NASCAR® and the NASCAR Library Collection® are registered
trademarks of the National Association for Stock Car Auto Racing, Inc.

www.eHarlequin.com

Printed in U.S.A.

NASCAR HIDDEN LEGACIES

The Grossos

Dean Grosso
m.
Patsy Clark Grosso

Patsy's brother

— Kent Grosso
(fiancée Tanya Wells)

— Gina Grosso
(deceased)

— Sophia Grosso
(fiancé Justin Murphy)

Dean's best friend

Business partner

The Clarks

Andrew Clark
(divorced)

Patsy's cousin

Kent's agent

Garrett Clark ⑯
(Andrew's stepson)

Jake McMasters ⑧

Kane Ledger ⑦

The Cargills

Alan Cargill (widower)

Nathan Cargill ⑤

The Claytons

Steve Clayton ⑩

— Mattie Clayton ⑭

Damon Tieri ⑪

The Branches

Maeve Branch
(div. Hilton Branch)
m.
Chuck Lawrence

— Will Branch ②

— Bart Branch

— Penny Branch m.
Craig Lockhart

— Sawyer Branch

① *Scandals and Secrets*
② *Black Flag, White Lies*
③ *Checkered Past*
④ *From the Outside*
⑤ *Over the Wall*
⑥ *No Holds Barred*
⑦ *One Track Mind*
⑧ *Within Striking Distance*
⑨ *Running Wide Open*
⑩ *A Taste for Speed*
⑪ *Force of Nature*
⑫ *Banking on Hope*
⑬ *The Comeback*
⑭ *Into the Corner*
⑮ *Raising the Stakes*
⑯ *Crossing the Line*

THE FAMILIES AND THE CONNECTIONS

The Sanfords

Bobby Sanford · · · · · · · · · · · · · ·
(deceased)
m.
Kath Sanford

— Adam Sanford ①

— Brent Sanford ⑫

— Trey Sanford ⑨

The Hunts

· · · · · · Dan Hunt
m.
Linda (Willard) Hunt
(deceased)

— Ethan Hunt ⑥

— Jared Hunt ⑮

— Hope Hunt ⑫

— Grace Hunt Winters ⑯
(widow of Todd Winters)

The Mathesons

Brady Matheson
(widower)
(fiancée Julie-Anne Blake)

— Chad Matheson ③

— Zack Matheson ⑬

— Trent Matheson
(fiancée Kelly Greenwood)

The Daltons

Buddy Dalton
m.
Shirley Dalton

— Mallory Dalton ④

— Tara Dalton ①

— Emma-Lee Dalton

CHAPTER ONE

"DADDY, I'M GETTING really hot in this dress. I'd like to go home, please."

Ethan Hunt looked down at his daughter's flushed, pleading face and decided he wanted the same thing she did. "We'll go soon, doodlebug," he promised. "When the band starts playing again we'll say our goodbyes and head out."

"Okay." Sadie pushed one of the frosting pansies from her piece of wedding cake around on her plate. "It's been fun and all, but—"

"It's time to get home and take care of your Zanies, right?" He was surprised he'd been able to talk Sadie out of bringing at least one of the fanciful stuffed animals and her handheld computer game to the wedding reception. She was seldom without one of the toys and the game of fantasy creatures she nurtured in their make-believe world.

Sadie perked up a bit. "Yes," she said. "I do need to get online before bedtime." She rested her chin on her hand and stared across the lawn at the bride and groom greeting well-wishers under a big live oak tree. "Sophia's wedding dress is so pretty. She looks just like a ballerina with that sparkly, swirly skirt and flowers in her hair."

"She's a very pretty bride," Ethan agreed. Sophia Grosso

and her groom, Justin Murphy's, Easter-weekend wedding and reception was being held on the lawn of Justin's Lake Norman home. The guest list was a who's who of NASCAR.

"Hey, Sadie, you look very pretty in that dress. Want to dance with me?" Trey Sanford asked, coming up to their table.

"Hi, Trey. No, I don't want to dance," Sadie said politely, not at all impressed she'd just been invited to dance by one of NASCAR's most eligible bachelors. "Thank you for saying my dress is pretty, but it's too hot."

"I hear you," Trey said, flipping a finger under the lapel of his sports jacket. "Really warm for April. Hi, Chief," he said, giving Ethan a half salute and a grin as he pulled a chair up to their tiny table, turned it around and straddled it, folding his arms on top of the backrest.

"Trey," Ethan acknowledged with a nod. Trey Sanford was the youngest brother of Ethan's boss, Adam Sanford, the owner of Sanford Racing, one of the oldest race teams in the business. He drove the No. 483 Greenstone Garden Centers car. Ethan was his crew chief.

"Where's Becky?" Sadie asked as Trey snatched some icing off Sadie's piece of cake and popped it in his mouth.

"She's around somewhere," Trey said, a frown etching a furrow between his eyebrows as he licked frosting off his fingers. "She'll show up when the music starts again." Ethan stopped worrying about the unsuitability of Sadie's velvet dress and focused his attention on the younger man. Trey and his fashion-model girlfriend, Becky Peters, had an on-again, off-again relationship, the ups and downs of which tended to affect his driving.

Trey didn't look too concerned at the moment, so

Ethan let himself relax. "C'mon," Trey coaxed. "Just one dance."

"Becky will dance with you when she gets back," Sadie pronounced around a mouthful of cake. "She's a good dancer."

The band struck up a lively country tune and a line dance began to form. Trey stood up. "Well, if you won't dance with me I'd better go find Becky before she has to come looking for me. See you at the shop, doodlebug."

"See you, Trey."

Sadie watched the handsome driver walk away. "Becky's thinking about breaking up with him again," she said matter-of-factly.

"What?"

Sadie's cheeks reddened a little. "I...I overheard her talking on the phone to her friend. I wasn't eavesdropping. She was talking to her in the car while we were driving to the shop. I couldn't help but listen."

"That's okay," Ethan said, slightly taken aback. Becky had been good enough to help him out by taking care of Sadie the past couple of days since the nanny he'd hired only a week earlier had broken her leg in two places. But he wasn't certain discussing her love life in front of an eleven-year-old was appropriate. Should he say something to Trey's girlfriend? He decided against it. After all, she had helped him out with Sadie as a friend, not an employee, but it only made him more anxious than ever to find a suitable nanny for his daughter.

"I like Becky. We had fun together. Look, there she is. She's pulling Trey out on the dance floor. They look really nice dancing together. Just like Barbie and Ken."

Ethan flicked a quick glance at his daughter. She was watching the dancing with a smile on her face. She meant it as a compliment, Ethan realized. She loved her Barbies and still kept them on prominent display in her bedroom, both the one at their home and at her grandparents', where she spent even more time during the racing season.

"They have trust issues, though," she said, looking very serious.

"Did she tell you that, too?"

"No. I saw it on *Oprah*. It was a show about couples that fight a lot. A guy and his girlfriend had the same kind of problems as Trey and Becky, except he was an insurance adjuster and she was a teacher. I figured it out from what they said. Do you think I should talk to Becky about it? I mean if she comes over to stay with me again?"

Ethan cleared his throat and didn't smile. "No," he said. "I think we should let them work it out for themselves."

"Yes, I imagine that's best," she said in a very grown-up voice.

Where did the kid get this stuff? Ethan wondered. She was always working out theories, thinking through the possibilities, coming up with fanciful and not so fanciful explanations for what made things tick. She wasn't a genius, but she did fall into the gifted category, and that was why he'd let his late wife's parents, Ford and Martha Pelton, talk him into sending her to the exclusive private school a few miles outside of Concord, North Carolina, where they lived. It was a good school and he didn't begrudge the high tuition fee, but it was also on a year-round class schedule and that was a real problem right at the moment. Sadie was on a six-week spring break that coincided with the month-long South American cruise that Ford and Martha had given each other as a fortieth-wedding-anniversary gift.

Martha had found a permanent nanny with impeccable references to take over for them, but when the woman broke her leg two days after Ford and Martha took off on their cruise, he had no backup for Sadie's care. He was on his own.

He hated to admit it, but he wasn't used to being a full-time parent. Laura's parents had always been there for him, and when Sadie had been small he'd justified their spending so much time with her as his effort to help assuage their grief over the loss of their only child. Since he'd taken over the crew chief's job at Sanford Racing, he had even less time for parenting than he had before.

He worked eighteen hours a day. He seldom slept in his own bed two nights in a row. He traveled four days out of seven, forty weeks of the year. Being a NASCAR Sprint Cup Series crew chief wasn't a nine-to-five kind of job. It was a 24/7 commitment. Especially when your driver was having a bad season like his was.

Trey Sanford was going through a rough patch. He'd been finishing in back of the pack most races this season, a tough pill to swallow after his great start at Daytona in February and his championship season in the NASCAR Nationwide Series the year before. Trey's patience was wearing thin. Hell, so was Ethan's but he didn't dare let it show. He was working on a tight budget, with a team that was beginning to show signs of strain and friction. He wondered some days how much longer his team owner, Adam Sanford, would put up with the situation before he started to make changes.

Adam wouldn't be firing his driver—his baby brother—that was for sure. Even if there were issues in Trey's life serious enough to bring Sanford Racing down with him.

The most logical person to go would be the guy who was supposed to hold the team together, call the shots, get the job done. In other words, the crew chief. One Ethan Daniel Hunt. Of course getting fired from his job would solve his other problem—not being there for his daughter. He'd have all the time in the world for Sadie then, and maybe that wasn't such a bad idea.

"Daddy, you're not eating your cake," Sadie remarked, eyeing his untouched piece. "Aren't you feeling well?"

"I'm fine, doodle," he said, pushing the piece of chocolate cake in her direction. "Just don't you make yourself sick eating too much frosting."

"I won't. In fact, I think I'll save it for lunch tomorrow."

Ethan felt his chest tighten with something akin to panic. Lunch tomorrow. Without a nanny to watch over her, he'd have to take her to the shop with him again. What would he do with her there all day? And the day after that? And the one after that? The agency better come through quickly.

"I was thinking we should stop in the kitchen and ask Aunt Grace if she has something to cover my cake with. I don't want to get frosting on the car seat."

"Good idea," Ethan praised her. "I should have thought of that."

Sadie beamed at the small compliment and he sucked in his breath. She had Laura's smile, and her eyes. Each day that passed she looked more and more like his late wife.

"We'll say our goodbyes to Justin and Sophia now," he said, standing up and holding out his hand for the plate of cake. "Then we can leave through the backyard and not get waylaid by anyone on our way to the car."

"Good," she said. "This has been fun. Especially the Easter-egg hunt and the piñata and everything. I didn't think there would be games for kids at a wedding reception. That was cool." He'd been surprised by how many children had attended the outdoor wedding and reception, and the activities the bride and her family had provided to entertain them. There were fifteen or twenty kids from toddlers to teenagers running between the tables, dancing with the grown-ups, stuffing their faces with cake and punch, and no one, least of all the bride and groom, seemed to mind.

Ethan glanced around the table-dotted lawn. All those people were making time for their families despite demanding careers of all kinds, not just NASCAR. He wanted Sadie with him full-time, not shuttling back and forth between two households like a little vagabond. He was beginning to suspect Ford and Martha, now heading into their seventies, wanted that, too. It was up to him to make it happen; he just wasn't sure how.

"Look. There's Justin and Sophia." Sadie held out her hand and he folded his own around it. She was small-boned and slender, but not fragile and prone to illness as Laura had been. She was stronger than she looked, and one of the things she'd inherited from him was a rock-solid constitution. She was almost never sick, thank heaven.

They caught up with the bride and groom as they were getting ready to take the dance floor, said their goodbyes and moved on toward the kitchen, where his adopted sister, Grace Winters, was overseeing her catering crew.

Grace's catering van, stenciled with her company name—

Gourmet by Grace—had been pulled close to the back door of the brick-and-frame house. Black-and-white-clad waiters moved back and forth, in and out, carrying trays of canapés to the tables, returning dirty flatware and dishes to the van, beginning to break down the steam tables and warming ovens they'd set up hours earlier.

"Hi, sis," Ethan said, giving Grace a quick wave.

"Hi, yourself," she called back, summoning one of her young assistants as she motioned for him to help her lift a large box into the van.

"I'll get that," Ethan said, taking a quick step forward, reaching for the heavy plastic tub before Grace could lift her end of it. "You'll ruin your dress." Ethan frowned as he and the youngster heaved the box into the back of the truck. Where was that slacker brother-in-law of hers? Tony Winters was supposed to be a partner in his sister's catering business. Supposed to be her right-hand man, but he was nowhere in sight.

As usual.

Ethan had been good friends with his late brother-in-law, Todd, but the dead man's older brother was another story altogether.

"Thanks, Ethan." She ignored his comment about ruining her dress and sent the young assistant on his way with a smile. "What are you two doing here?" she asked, wiping her hands on the big white apron that covered her from neck to knee. She wasn't wearing chef's whites, or even utilitarian black and white like her staff. She was dressed in some gauzy, summery pink dress that brought out the gold in her hair and the blue in her eyes, because she was supposed to be dancing and drinking champagne out there on the lawn with the other invited guests, not loading a truck.

Ethan opened his mouth to say just that, but she gave a slight shake of her head and a wave of her hand, warning him off. "I'll talk to him," she said, almost reading his mind, as she so often did. They'd been close ever since her mother had first brought the tiny, golden-haired three-year-old to their house when Linda and his dad, Dan, started dating. Ethan had been eleven and it had been love at first sight. She'd been his baby sister, his favorite, from that day forward, even after his half sister, Hope, arrived some years later.

"Aunt Grace, I need a take-out box," Sadie explained, showing Grace her piece of cake.

"We can arrange that." She flagged down another of her helpers and gave the red-faced girl instructions. "LaDeena will fix you up. Sit with me until she gets back." She motioned to a nearby cedar picnic table and took a seat herself with a little sigh of relief. "My feet hurt," she said, sliding out of her pumps. "These are definitely not the shoes for catering three hundred guests."

"That's because they're dancing shoes," Sadie pointed out.

"Since we're on the subject, why aren't you dancing?" Ethan asked, aware his frown was arching a deep furrow in his forehead. "Why are you back here and not out front? You're a guest, too."

"I'm also the owner of this business," she reminded him. "The buck stops here."

"Where's Tony? Isn't this what he's supposed to be doing? The grunt work? You're the talent. He's the brawn, right?"

"More or less," she said, frowning slightly. "Something came up. Susan's not feeling well."

"Susan's always not feeling well these days," he commented. Susan was Todd and Tony's mother, Grace's mother-in-law.

"I know and it worries me. Susan misses our mom as much as we do." Linda Hunt had died suddenly of an undetected cancer in November, and the loss was still hard for all of them to accept. The red-faced girl returned with a foam take-out box and handed it to Grace.

"Thanks, LaDeena." Grace sent the girl on her way with another smile.

"Hey, isn't she supposed to be scared witless around you? Aren't you supposed to make her quake in her boots?"

Ethan watched the cooking shows on TV. He didn't have much choice. Half the guys on the team seemed to be addicted to the cooking channels and the do-it-yourself channels on the cable stations, and spent their downtime on the road watching them. He knew how celebrity chefs were supposed to act, yelling and cussing and throwing tantrums all over their kitchens.

"That gets me about as far as you cussing out all the floor guys at the shop. And besides, it gives me a headache." Grace didn't berate her staff or browbeat them into submission. She got what she wanted out of them by leading by example, by working twice as hard and twice as long as any of them.

"Would you like a care package for lunch tomorrow?" Grace asked Sadie. "Are you going to the shop with your dad?"

"Yes," Sadie answered, nodding, "for the whole day."

The exchange between his sister and daughter pulled him out of his thoughts. Sadie at the race shop. All day tomorrow and every day after that. The worry kicked back in at full bore. She was safe enough in his office, but he didn't spend a whole lot of time behind his desk. How was he going to keep her occupied all those hours there alone? The agency that had found the nanny for Martha had promised to send over a prospect as soon as possible, but he didn't have much hope it would be before seven the next morning.

His worrying thoughts must have shown on his face because Grace stopped smiling and regarded him solemnly. "Sadie, why don't you go into the kitchen and ask LaDeena to fix you some goodies to take home for lunch tomorrow? Whatever you like. There's plenty of food left."

"Thanks, Aunt Grace. Can I have another piece of cake, too? I was starving at the garage the other day. They don't have anything good in the vending machines, and Dad was too busy to take me out to lunch." She danced away toward the kitchen door.

"What am I going to do with her, sis?" Ethan asked. "Her school break couldn't have come at a worse time."

"You'll think of something," Grace said, with an encouraging smile, but unfortunately it didn't quite banish the doubt from her eyes.

"There's nothing for her to do at the garage," he said, watching Sadie disappear through the screen door into the kitchen. "There's evidently not even anything for her to eat."

"She's got her laptop and there's a TV in your office. It's not as if you're locking her in a dark closet. Lighten up. The agency will come through with a new nanny. And she'll be with me and the kids when you leave for Phoenix."

"I owe you big-time for that, too. I can't be stashing her in motel rooms and motor homes half the time." He looked down between his legs unable to meet her eyes because he knew old sorrows lurked there that mirrored his own. "It wasn't supposed to be like this, Gracie. You and Todd. Me and Laura. We weren't supposed to have to do this alone."

"We're not alone. We have Dad and I have Susan. Ford and Martha are there for you. We're here for each other, and our brother, Jared, will help out in a pinch."

"I've let Ford and Martha take too many of my responsibilities on their shoulders the last few years."

"When you're a single parent you do the best you can."

"That's easy enough for you to say. I missed all the team meetings, all the memos. I'm starting from the back of the pack with this parenting thing, and I'm afraid that Sadie's the one who's going to suffer for it."

CHAPTER TWO

"WHAT DO YOU MEAN you didn't get offered the mechanic's job at Sanford Racing?" Lelah Connors asked her youngest daughter.

"Chief Hunt was very nice about it," Mia replied. "He said my work was excellent during my internship, but they just didn't have the budget for another mechanic right now."

"The way Trey Sanford's been driving since Daytona I'm surprised Ethan Hunt hasn't been fired from *his* job."

"Mom, you're not helping." Cassie Connors folded her arms across her chest, leaned her hips against the kitchen sink to take some of the pressure off her damaged right leg and looked across the chipped Formica table at her younger sister. "At your evaluation two weeks ago you said Ethan Hunt practically promised you a full-time job when your NASCAR Technical Institute internship ended."

Mia's lips tightened as she tried to keep from crying. "He did. But since then, Trey lost one of the car's associate sponsors. You know with all that gossip about him making late-night flights to Mexico to meet some woman and all. It's a very conservative sponsor. They don't like that kind of story leaking out, even if it isn't true. No one is supposed to know," Mia said, glancing between her mother and sister. "Please don't say anything."

Mia was nineteen, just graduated from the NASCAR Technical Institute in Mooresville, North Carolina, a freshly certified NASCAR mechanic. At five-five she was two inches taller than Cassie. Her brown hair was shorter and didn't owe its blond highlights to a bottle. They had the same snub nose, the same heart-shaped face and hazel eyes, the same softly rounded feminine curves. Curves that in Cassie's case were ruthlessly controlled by exercise and avoidance of everything chocolate, but the resemblance ended there. Cassie was nine years older and ten pounds heavier than Mia, and she had eight years of service in the United States Marine Corps under her belt, including a tour of duty in Iraq.

"He probably started making calls the minute the door closed behind you," Lelah remarked bitterly. She was a small woman, nearing fifty, petite and fine-boned, built along the same lines as her daughters. And she'd once been just as pretty and carefree as Mia, Cassie knew from old photos. But a failed marriage, constant money worries and the chronic pain of rheumatoid arthritis had leeched the prettiness from her face and the spring from her step.

Cassie tightened her jaw but kept silent. She tended to agree with her mother's assessment of Ethan Hunt, although to be fair she'd never met the man. She'd run into enough of that kind in the military, though, to last her a lifetime.

"No, he wouldn't do that," Mia defended her boss. "I believe he's telling the truth about the team not being able to make any new hires. It's hard times for the smaller teams in racing these days. Besides," Mia said, looking down at her hands and not at her mother and sister as she spoke, "he offered me another job, instead."

"At the shop?" Cassie was suddenly glad she hadn't badmouthed Ethan Hunt out loud. Maybe she had him pegged wrong, after all? She shouldn't let her experience with desk jockeys in the corps or her jerk of a former boss color her opinion of every other man out there.

"Not exactly," Mia hedged, raising her gaze but not quite meeting Cassie's eyes.

"Mia Lynette Connors. The man didn't proposition you, did he?" Lelah sputtered. "That's sexual harassment. We should call the police…or…somebody."

"He didn't proposition me, Mom. He's thirty-six or thirty-seven if he's a day. Too old for me." Mia reflected a moment. "But for Cassie, now…I mean, he's kind of hot, actually. He's got really broad shoulders and a good-looking butt—"

"Mia. What job did he offer you?" Cassie interrupted. Lelah's eyes had grown big as saucers hearing her baby girl talk like that about a man's backside.

"He needs a nanny for his little girl. Someone to watch over her while he's at the shop."

"A nanny." Lelah threw up her hands. "We didn't spend the last of my inheritance from your grandmother to pay your way through NASCAR Tech so you could be a nanny to some spoiled brat."

"Sadie's not a spoiled brat," Mia said, her chin coming up. "She's a cute kid. Lonely and a little sad, and too quiet, maybe, but not a brat. She's smart as a whip, too. Her name is Mercedes, Sadie for short. She spends a lot of time with her grandparents, but they're on a cruise around South

America and the nanny Chief Hunt hired for her broke her leg tripping over her cat. He's desperate to have someone look after her. The agency he uses doesn't have anyone available."

"What did you tell him?" Cassie asked, topping off her mother's glass of sweet tea before sitting down beside Mia. She was curious to hear her sister's response, although she suspected she already knew the answer.

Mia shrugged slightly, her disappointment showing through her brave front for a moment. "I said yes," she responded. "Sadie's a nice kid. Besides, I need the job. Mom didn't have to remind me how much in hock we are for my education. I know the total to the penny."

Remorse brought quick tears to Lelah's eyes. She placed her hand over Mia's. "I'm sorry I said that. I didn't mean to hurt your feelings. It's only money. We'll get by."

Cassie winced inwardly. That had been Lelah's mantra as long as she could remember. Only now the responsibility for "getting by" in the Connors family fell to her. For the past two years, ever since she'd been given a medical discharge from the Marine Corps after suffering shrapnel wounds when an IED—improvised explosive device—had hit the truck she was riding in, she'd been working as an office manager at an architectural firm. Unfortunately now she was unemployed. Her former boss, taken to the cleaners by his long-suffering wife's divorce lawyer, had locked the office door behind him and set off to find his inner balance in a monastery in Nepal without first bothering to write a letter of recommendation for his equally long-suffering office staff.

"I'm just so disappointed for you." Lelah sniffed.

"Doesn't that man have any idea how good a mechanic he turned down? You were top of your class. You outscored every man in the program. He could be making history hiring you. The woman destined to be the first female crew chief in NASCAR." Again Lelah threw up her hands, exaggerating every gesture, trying to coax Mia into a better humor.

"I kind of have my sights set on car chief, not crew chief. Too much pressure even if some of them make the big bucks," Mia said, attempting a smile. Cassie watched as her young sister pushed aside her own disappointment to spare Lelah as much stress as possible. It was a habit they'd both learned early in life.

"Sadie's a great kid. I won't mind babysitting her. If I can't get a job with a NASCAR Sprint Cup team, maybe I'll make a name for myself as the famous Super-Nanny, babysitter to the stars of stock car racing." Mia gave a hiccupping little sob and two tears rolled down her cheeks. The false bravado drained from her voice. "But I really, really wanted this job with Sanford Racing. I really did."

Cassie had been looking out for her sister since Mia was five and Cassie fourteen and their footloose father had taken off never to be heard from again. Mia might be almost grown-up and on her own, but Cassie still felt responsible for her. And she hated to see her cry. She pushed away from the table and stood up. "I'll be back in an hour or so," she said, adrenaline pumping through her bloodstream, urging her to action. "I've got some things I have to do."

"ETHAN? DO YOU HAVE a moment?" Maria Salinas's voice sounded hesitant as it came through the intercom speaker on his desk.

"What is it?" Ethan winced at the impatience in his voice. It wasn't the Sanford Racing receptionist's fault he was in a bad mood. Adam Sanford had just shot down his request for an extra weekend of wind tunnel testing. Too expensive. Nothing left in the budget this season for an unscheduled test session, he'd said.

Money. It always came down to money these days. Money—or the lack of it. Sure, his team owner had provided him with some of the best software available but at the end of the day computer simulations, no matter how sophisticated, didn't take the place of a driver behind the wheel of his car. He needed Trey's input for the next phase of retooling his underperforming car—up close and personal, butt in the seat, hands on the wheel, not sitting in front of a big-screen TV playing high-tech video games.

"You have a visitor." There was an odd note in Maria's tone, as though she were torn between laughing and calling for help, that focused his attention in a hurry.

"I don't have any more appointments for today," he said. "Get their name and tell them I'll call them later if it's important."

"I don't think this lady is going to take no for an answer." There was a short, charged moment of silence and then Maria's voice, from a distance, calling, "Wait. You can't go in there."

Ethan didn't even have time to hang up the phone before the door swung open unceremoniously and Mia Connors entered his office for the second time that day.

He blinked and took another look. No, it wasn't Mia Connors, but someone obviously closely related to his daughter's new nanny. This woman was slightly shorter, slightly heavier with curves in all the right places. Her hair was darker than Mia's, as well, a rich golden brown that waved softly around her shoulders, held back from her face by a pair of tortoiseshell combs. And her eyes. They were different, too, hazel with flecks of gold and green and brown floating in their depths, just slightly elongated at the edges, giving her a faintly feline look, sleek, well fed, purring contentedly on your lap—until you crossed her.

He was looking at Mia's older sister, he guessed, the former Marine. What was her name? Carrie? Cathie? Something that started with a *C*.

"Ethan Hunt?" she said in a forceful tone, banishing any further resemblance to a placid tabby. "I'm Cassandra Connors, Mia Connors's sister. I'd like to talk to you, if I may." She stood very straight, her shoulders back, her jaw thrust forward. She was wearing a calf-length, flowered cotton skirt and a short-sleeved V-neck sweater in a color he could best describe as kind of strawberry red. It just matched the angry flush on her cheeks.

"What can I do for you, Ms. Connors?" From the look on her face she wasn't here to heap praise on his head for hiring her sister.

"I'm here to ask you why you withdrew your offer to my sister of a job as a mechanic here at the race shop."

He was right. She was here to do battle for her little sister. He couldn't fault her for that. He had done battle for both his sisters in the past.

"Won't you have a seat, Ms. Connors?" he asked.

"No, thank you. What I want is for you to reconsider your earlier decision."

"I'm afraid that's not possible."

"Why not? I'm not an expert on NASCAR, but it seems to me a certified NASCAR mechanic and a child's nanny are not interchangeable job descriptions. Am I correct, sir?"

"You are correct."

"My sister needs to be looking for a job in her chosen field, not helping you out of a jam by babysitting your daughter while you dangle the *possibility* of hiring her somewhere down the line." Her tone was perfectly even and devoid of heat, but the emphasis on the word was unmistakable.

"Mia's employment has been exemplary. We're happy with her work," he said. "Unfortunately Sanford Racing is not hiring at this particular time."

She ignored his compliment on her sister's work ethic. "Where is your daughter?"

He was a little riled himself now. The Marine Corps mascot was a bulldog, he recalled suddenly. It was certainly an appropriate symbol for this particular Marine. "She's in the break room having a snack. Not that it's any of your business."

"On the contrary," she said, not backing down an inch. "Since you coerced my sister into taking a job as her nanny, it is my business."

"I did not coerce your sister into anything," he responded, ignoring the tug of his conscience as he spoke. He hadn't coerced Mia, not exactly. She was an exemplary employee and a damned good mechanic. He'd have hired her permanently in a heartbeat if he could have. He wasn't proud of himself for manipulating the girl into becoming Sadie's nanny, but he was a desperate man. "The long and short of it is Sanford Racing doesn't have an opening for a mechanic at this time," he said bluntly.

"Then that makes what you did even worse. You have no intention of ever hiring my sister into this shop, correct?"

"I did not say that, Ms. Connors. I intend to keep my word to Mia. I want her on the team. I thought my suggestion would be a solution to both our problems, continued employment for Mia, a responsible nanny for my daughter. She agreed to the proposition." It was time to end this discussion before it escalated into an argument. He couldn't believe how this woman was pushing his buttons. He never let that happen. A gentleman didn't argue with a woman. He remembered his mother, his real mother, telling him that, in her soft, whispery voice. "Mia accepted my offer of her own free will. If she's changed her mind, then I need to hear that from her own mouth. Now, if you'll excuse me, Ms. Connors. I'll see you to the door. I have work to do."

HE WASN'T GOING to get rid of her that easily. Cassie took a step closer to Ethan Hunt's big metal desk and leaned her hands on the scratched and dented surface. "What kind of father are you?" she asked, her heart beating hard and fast in her chest. *Panic. It was only an inch or two from breaking out, but she wasn't going to give in to it this time. She wasn't in any danger. Neither was anyone else.* She could get through this. She would for Mia's sake. "My sister is too young to make this decision on her own. She is only thinking of the short-term consequences of being unemployed. She needs to be concentrating on breaking into NASCAR. She can't do that babysitting your daughter." The incipient panic receded into the corner of her mind where she kept it caged, but as the adrenaline rush that had propelled her across town and into the office of

Sanford Racing's crew chief also faded, she began to wonder if she couldn't have handled this confrontation more diplomatically.

"Again the decision is up to Mia, not to you." It was apparent he was holding on to his temper with some difficulty.

Cassie shook her head. "She'd never say no to you, so I'm doing it for her. I trust you are enough of a gentleman not to refuse to write her a reference when she needs one."

Ethan Hunt stood up then, and she had to give up the territory she'd taken in her advance across his office just to be able to meet his gaze without tilting her head. He was a formidable presence, she thought, assessing the enemy. Broad shoulders, big hands, a square jaw and eyes the same shade of blue as the deepest ocean water. He probably weighed 180 dripping wet and not one ounce of it was fat. *Dripping wet.* She caught herself before the words could morph into a mental image that she knew would bring heat to her face—and farther down, low in her belly—which shocked her almost as much as her lascivious thoughts about the man in the first place.

"I admit I might have pressed Mia a bit too hard to agree to the plan, Ms. Connors." His voice was steel-hard beneath his slow Carolina drawl. "But that last remark was uncalled for."

He was right. She had gone over the line. "I…I apologize," Cassie said, swallowing. She began to consider her options for a tactical retreat. She took a deep breath. "I tend to go off half-cocked sometimes. Please forgive me."

"Even after eight years of Marine Corps discipline?"

"Yes. How did you know that I spent eight years in the corps?" she asked suspiciously.

"Mia, of course. She's very proud of you." Ethan Hunt narrowed his eyes. "Sit down, Ms. Connors," he said abruptly, indicating one of the two leather chairs in front of his desk. Used to obeying orders barked in that particular tone of voice, Cassie sat. "Perhaps there's a way out of this dilemma for both of us."

"What do you mean?"

"I mean if Mia is turning down the job as my daughter's nanny because you want her to, then perhaps I should offer the position to you, instead?"

"What do you mean?" She felt the panic stir again and slammed the mental door that caged it shut with a bang. Taking care of a child? Responsible for her safety and welfare? She wasn't ready for that.

"Would you take the job in her place if I could figure out a way to keep Mia on here at Sanford Racing?"

"I…" He had dangled the one bait in front of her she couldn't resist. *Could she handle it? She just couldn't be sure. Better safe than sorry.* "Don't be ridiculous," she said so sharply she caught herself by surprise. "You don't know me from Adam. I…I could be an ax murderer. A raving lunatic…" She almost choked on the words. She wasn't either of those things, but she did suffer from post-traumatic stress disorder, and although her panic attacks were far less severe and of shorter duration these past months than they had been when she first returned from overseas, she didn't know if she was ready to take charge of a child's welfare.

"I doubt it," Ethan Hunt said with an alarmingly sensual grin. "Mooresville is a small town. I'd have heard about any ax murders." He sat down again and began tapping on the keyboard he'd been working at when she burst into the office. She couldn't see the screen of his monitor from where she sat, but he stared at it intently. "Sanford Racing isn't in the same league with Maximus Motorsports or Cargill-Grosso Racing, but we're not exactly dirt track around here, either. Here we go," he said. "Cassandra Cecelia Connors. Age 28. Five feet three inches tall. One hundred and twenty pounds. I would have guessed a tad more," he said without looking up from the screen.

Cassie opened her mouth to object, but no words came out.

"Address—323 Portsmouth Street, Mooresville, North Carolina. Same as Mia's, of course. Not the worst neighborhood in town," he commented, still not looking at her.

"Not the best," she muttered back.

"I grew up about six blocks farther away from the mill. My dad still lives in the same house."

"Your father's Dan Hunt," she said. "He was a NASCAR crew chief, wasn't he?" She couldn't remember which team Dan Hunt had been associated with. She didn't follow stock car racing as closely as her mother and sister did, but she'd picked up a few details about the Hunts and Sanfords by osmosis since Mia secured the coveted internship at Sanford Racing.

His eyes remained focused on the screen. "My dad was Alan Cargill's crew chief. He's retired now. Are you a race fan?"

She shrugged. "Not as much as some people. My uncle used to race dirt track. I went to high school with Sophia Grosso. That's about the extent of it."

"I didn't see you at the wedding yesterday."

"We weren't that close," she said tightly. "I didn't run

with the same crowd." The cool kids, the rich kids, she let her tone imply.

To her surprise he looked a bit sheepish. "Sure. I understand."

"Doesn't your fancy security program tell you all that? So far all the information you've given me you could have gotten from my driver's license."

He ignored her jab. "You and Mia live with your mother."

"Correct."

"Lelah Kelsey Connors. Fifty on her next birthday. Unemployed. Seems not to have held a job for some years."

"My mother suffers from rheumatoid arthritis. She is unable to work outside our home."

"That would explain it," he said. "You are unemployed, as well, at the moment."

She tensed, then deliberately made herself relax. Okay, his information was more detailed than she thought. "My boss was fooling around on his wife. When she found out she took him for everything he had. He closed his firm and took off for Nepal to find himself without bothering to write references for the staff, myself included." What was she doing? Name. Rank and serial number. That was all the Geneva Convention required a prisoner of war to give her captors. Or an overbearing NASCAR crew chief.

"What did you do for this…seeker of truth?"

"I managed his office. Everything from soup to nuts. Payroll to travel schedules. I was good at it, too." She stood up. "Look, Mr. Hunt, you've made your point. I don't need to hear any more. I changed my mind about Mia taking the job. I won't put any more obstacles in your path. She will make your daughter a good nanny."

He glanced over at her, ignoring her last speech. "You made sergeant after only three years in the corps. Impressive."

"I was good at what I did. And there was lots of opportunity for advancement in Iraq," she said, closing her lips before she added the automatic and ingrained "sir."

"You were in Iraq during the roughest time," he continued without looking up from the screen.

"Yes." She tensed. Maybe his program wasn't just a portal to the Department of Motor Vehicles. Maybe he would be able to access her medical information. Then he would know she had spent six months in therapy for the panic attacks she was only just now getting under control. Her palms began to sweat. She rubbed them surreptitiously on her skirt.

"You received a letter of Commendation for Valor."

"I was only doing my job." Not exactly. She had "gone outside the wire," against regulations for female Marines, when she'd taken a spot in one of the big lumbering trucks that delivered supplies to forward units in the field. She'd put herself in harm's way so that she could take care of her guys, her Marines. The sergeant who usually pulled that duty was down with some kind of nasty stomach bug, so she'd stepped up. That was all.

"You received a Purple Heart." His eyebrows had climbed toward his hairline.

"We were ambushed. It happened a lot over there." Forced off the road by a suicide driver, the truck ahead of them had triggered an IED and exploded. Cassie had been wounded by shrapnel and suffered nerve damage to her right leg. And later, after she was home safe and sound, the nightmares and panic attacks associated with post-traumatic stress disorder had begun.

"I thought women weren't allowed in combat zones," he said, pushing the keyboard away, resting his hands on the top of his desk. His hard face revealed little emotion, but she saw something flicker behind his eyes, respect and admiration. She sat a little straighter in her chair.

"The situation was fluid," she said. "I was just doing my job."

"It's a hell of a world where women have to fight in wars."

"I'm a United States Marine who happens to be a woman. I was doing what I was trained to do." It was time to change the subject. "We're not here to talk about what happened to me. We're here to talk about your daughter and my sister."

He nodded. "Okay. I'll make you a deal," he said. "Do you like children?"

"Yes, of course I do." A flutter of regret squeezed her heart. She had always wanted children of her own, but that was before. Before Iraq and the panic attacks she feared more than combat.

"You helped raise Mia, didn't you?"

"Yes. Our father walked out on us when I was fourteen. But I don't see—" She closed her mouth and stood up. What was he up to now? She didn't intend to answer any more personal questions from this man. She could leave right now if she wanted to. She was in control of her own actions.

"Mia's fantastic. If you helped raise her, then I think you'd be a great nanny for my Sadie. I repeat—I'm offering you the same job I offered your sister two hours ago." He held up a restraining hand. "Hear me out. If you agree to take over the responsibility for my daughter's care, I'll hire your sister into the shop. I can't guarantee she'll get to work on the cars all that much. I was telling you the truth when I said we didn't need another mechanic right now. But I'll see to it she's got something to do with race cars. Deal?" he asked, staring directly into her eyes.

She hadn't obtained the rank of sergeant in less than three years because of a lack of initiative. She was backed into a corner and didn't see any way of talking herself out of it. He knew he'd offered her the one option she couldn't turn down, a chance for Mia to continue working at Sanford Racing.

The navy shrinks had told her she was doing great, that it was time for her to move on with her life, get on with her future. She was ready. But she hadn't been so sure. Now she didn't have any choice but to make the attempt.

For Mia's sake if not for her own.

Cassie took a deep breath and felt as if she was stepping off the edge of a cliff. "Deal," she said, praying that she wasn't making a mistake both she and this man—and his little girl—would regret. "You've got yourself a deal."

He held out his hand. "Excellent," he said. "And by the way, thank you for your service to our country."

CHAPTER THREE

"THIS IS THE HOUSE," Sadie declared, consulting the address Ethan had jotted down on a slip of paper. "And we're right on time."

They were having dinner with Cassie Connors and her family. He wasn't sure exactly how it had happened, but Cassie had insisted that Sadie should have a chance to give her opinion on the switch from Mia to Cassie as her new companion—not nanny; apparently Sadie was too old for a nanny—and inspect the place where she'd be spending a lot of time over the next several weeks. He had agreed, because he didn't see he had much choice. "It's not very big, is it?"

He glanced over at his daughter's profile as he maneuvered his 4x4 to the curb in front of the modest frame house. He wondered if Sadie had ever before been in a neighborhood like this one, respectable but a little run-down and worn around the edges. Ford and Martha were not rich, by any means, but Ford had worked hard all his life and done well with his investments, and the other students at his daughter's private school were far more well-to-do than he and Sadie's grandparents combined.

"They have a dog!" Sadie whispered ecstatically,

pointing out the window. "Cassie and Mia have a dog. There. See it? Looking at us out of the window. Oh, see that adorable little bow in its fur? I can't wait to pet her."

She wouldn't notice now if they walked into an igloo plunked down in the middle of this street of similar, two-story frame houses. She would only have eyes for the dog. Sadie wanted a pet badly. Martha suffered from a number of respiratory ailments, so there were no pets at her grandparents' home. But his house was big. And the yard was huge. Maybe it was time he got her a dog?

"Dad, come on. Turn off the truck so I can take off my seat belt." Sadie reached over and tapped his arm to get his attention. She was conscientious about details like that. She would be conscientious about caring for a pet, too—a real one, not cyber. Would Sgt. Cassie Connors, former U.S. Marine, consider housebreaking a puppy to be outside her duties as Sadie's new companion? Dog-sitting hadn't been mentioned in their unconventional job interview that morning.

He switched off the ignition, undid his own seat belt and climbed out of the truck in time to catch Sadie as she got ready to jump off the running board. He swung her up in the air and set her on her feet, pretending to be breathless from the effort. "You're getting too big for me to do that, doodlebug," he said, although she'd felt light as a feather in his arms.

"I hope not," she surprised him by saying. "I like it when you swing me up like that. It's almost like flying. When I was little you did fly me like an airplane, up and down, around in circles." She held out her arms. "Mama would laugh and laugh. I remember."

"I remember, too," Ethan said. His daughter had so few

memories of Laura. He hoped this particular one didn't fade over time.

Sadie tugged on his hand. "Stop scowling. They'll think you don't like their house," she whispered, looking concerned.

"That's not why I'm frowning, but I'll quit." He put his own memories aside and pasted a big silly grin on his face. "How's that?"

She studied him for a moment, as if he was serious. "No. Don't like that, either. I like your real smile. You just don't do it enough."

On those deflating words they reached the wire gate in the fence that separated the tiny front yard from the street and sidewalk. The narrow walkway to the house was lined with pots of flowers and vegetables, and two steps beyond that, just inside the screen door, a pint-sized Yorkie with a camouflage-patterned bow in its hair, barked furiously.

"Puddles. Stand down." Cassie's voice was calm but commanding. The small dog gave one last excited yap in their direction and disappeared from the screen door. "Hello, Sadie." Cassie smiled at his daughter as she held open the door. "It's nice to meet you."

"Thank you for inviting us for dinner," Sadie said politely.

"We're very glad you could come. I thought it would be nice if we got to know each other a little better before we're left alone together all day," Cassie said, still smiling. She held out her hand to Sadie. "I hope it's okay that you'll be spending time with me and not Mia."

Sadie hesitated a moment before clasping Cassie's hand, unused to being treated in such a grown-up manner. "I like Mia a lot. We have lunch together at the shop sometimes and talk about all kinds of things. There aren't all that many women working in NASCAR Sprint Cup shops, you know."

"I know."

There weren't all that many women serving in combat units, either, Ethan thought. The sisters had their unconventional choice of occupations in common, as well as the self-esteem and confidence it took to be successful in a male-dominated profession.

"You're older, though, aren't you?" Sadie asked with devastating frankness.

"Yes," Cassie responded. "I'm afraid I am."

He hadn't gone to the break room to get Sadie when Cassie had invaded his office because it had all transpired so quickly it hadn't entered his head that his daughter might object to being given a second nanny in under two hours. Not, that is, until Cassie tossed out her invitation— no, *challenge* was a better word—for the two of them to come here for dinner, to meet her and her mother, and see where Sadie would be spending a great share of each day.

"How old are you?"

"Sadie, that's not polite."

"I'm twenty-eight," Cassie said. "But I'm not totally lame. You can ask Mia." He watched Cassie closely, seeking clues to her personality as she conversed with his daughter. Her smile looked a little forced now, as though she was more nervous about this meeting than Sadie was. "And if you don't like what you see, just say so and the deal's off."

"Now wait a moment," Ethan sputtered. He had agreed to the meeting, not to giving Sadie veto power over the arrangement.

Cassie straightened her shoulders, the not-quite-standing-at-attention thing again. "Sadie should have a say in the matter." Her tone left no room for argument. "I've invited you here so that she can check us out as thoroughly as you've investigated my family." She held the screen door a little wider. "Please, Sadie. Come on in."

Sadie stepped into the house without another moment's hesitation, drawing him along in her wake. "May I pet your dog?" she asked as the small terrier hopped down off the back of the couch, where it had been observing them with bright, excited eyes.

"Yes. Just give him a moment to get used to you," Cassie cautioned as the little Yorkie bounced over to sniff at Sadie's shoes and then at the hand she held out, fingers curled under in case the dog forgot his manners and nipped—something she picked up on *Animal Planet,* Ethan supposed.

"There's a bow in his fur. Why does a boy dog have a bow in his fur?" Puddles had jumped up to rest his forepaws on Sadie's leg, demanding to be petted. She obliged, bending down to scratch behind his ears.

"It's to keep his hair out of his eyes. And it's a camouflage bow. Very masculine, don't you think?" Cassie asked, looking at Ethan, a smile tipping up the corners of her mouth. He felt a little zing of excitement course through his veins.

"Fashionable and functional. Not bad," he croaked, surprised by his reaction to her.

She had a very pretty mouth, he realized. And those eyes, more green than hazel, the color of a stream beneath a willow, golden flecks of sunshine dancing on the surface and deep into their depths. He hadn't noticed the color of a woman's eyes that way…well, for a long, long time. He had trouble looking away for a moment. Too long, evidently.

"Get down," she ordered.

"I'm sorry," he apologized automatically.

"Not you. Puddles."

Following her line of sight, Ethan looked down. Puddles had lifted a hind leg, getting ready to take aim at his shoe. From out of nowhere Mia Connors pounced on the little dog and scooped him out the front door. "Oh, no, you don't. No peeing on my boss's shoe."

Sadie put her hand over her mouth. Cassie groaned. Color rushed to her cheeks and for a moment she actually looked younger than Mia. "I'm so sorry," she said. "He hasn't done that in ages."

"There hasn't been a man in this house in ages," Mia muttered.

"Dad, he was going to pee on your shoe," Sadie said. "Just like you were a tree or a bush." She burst out in giggles and after a moment Cassie followed suit.

"That's why we named him Puddles." She caught Sadie's eye and his daughter giggled again.

"Good one," she said, smiling at Cassie. "That's a good one."

Mia closed the door firmly on the Yorkie's offended howls and offered Ethan her hand. "Thank you for extending my internship," she said. "I'll work my butt off."

Ethan returned the handshake. "When I explained the situation to Mr. Sanford, he agreed to the plan. You realize I can't promise you anything beyond the end of the season, though."

"Don't worry. By the end of the season I'll be indispensable to the team," she said, grinning. "I'll be at the shop 24/7 if you need me."

Ethan kept his expression businesslike, but inwardly he approved of her confident manner. Adam Sanford understood what a bind he was in finding someone to care for Sadie so he could concentrate on getting Trey and his underperforming car to Victory Lane, and had agreed to Ethan's scheme when he proposed it to him a short time earlier.

"Mr. Hunt, this is my mother, Lelah Connors," Cassie said as an older woman entered the room.

"How do you do, Mrs. Connors."

"Welcome to our home, Mr. Hunt." She moved slowly into the small living room, her left hand resting on the head of a wooden cane. Her fingers were bent and twisted. Her face, once as pretty as her daughters', he guessed, was lined with pain. She was a small, birdlike woman seemingly light enough to blow over in a strong breeze.

He always felt oversize and awkward around women like Lelah Connors. He had felt that way, too, sometimes, with Laura, even though she used to laugh and tell him he was ridiculous to think he might harm her if they made love too exuberantly. Odd that he should recall that particular memory now. He hadn't thought of making love, barely thought of sex at all, for a long, long time. Until today.

Until he met Cassie Connors.

"I THINK THAT WENT pretty well," Mia said, drying the last of the plates Cassie had just washed, then putting it in the cupboard.

"Sadie had two helpings of spaghetti," Lelah said from

her seat at the table, a cup of coffee cradled between her ruined hands. "She said it was the best she'd ever had."

"The sauce came out of a jar, Mom," Cassie teased. "Most kids like spaghetti." Her Marines, most of them Mia's age or younger, would load up on it in the chow line, or pick it out of the boxes of MREs—meals ready to eat— that sometimes constituted her entire day's rations when her unit was making deliveries of supplies and bottled water to the forward bases.

"Ethan didn't eat much," Mia observed.

He had insisted they call him Ethan. He'd directed that remark to Lelah with a smile that had just about knocked Cassie off her feet, and it had only caught her a glancing blow as it ricocheted around the room. She figured she might have found herself flat on the floor if he'd aimed it directly at her.

It had started slow and spread across his face, deepening the lines at the corners of his mouth and his eyes, darkening them to the color of the sky before a summer storm. Where had it come from, that smile, hinting at sin and sex and lovemaking in the middle of a soft Southern night? Her toes curled just thinking about it. She had thought the man a cold fish at first. But when he smiled? Well, that was another animal entirely.

And he was sneaky. Somehow in the ninety minutes he and Sadie had been inside the house he'd maneuvered her into agreeing that it would be best if she came to his house in the country to care for Sadie.

How had that happened?

She wasn't quite sure. One minute they had been sitting around the table, eating ice cream and talking about the lovely weather that had prevailed over the holiday weekend when Sadie mentioned that her dad had a pool at his house and it was heated.

Without a moment's hesitation or a word of consultation, he had altered the terms of her employment. It shouldn't have come as such a surprise, Cassie realized. That was what a crew chief did on a NASCAR team. He may have planned a different strategy, but when an opportunity opened up, you took it. Strategize or improvise, but above all else, act. He would have made a good Marine.

"You know," he had said, "now that I think about it, why don't you come out to my place to watch over Sadie? All her things are there. And she's right. There is a pool. A big one. And it's heated." He'd turned that damned smile on Lelah then. "And you must come, too, Mrs. Connors," he'd insisted. "My late mother's aunt has rheumatoid arthritis. She says swimming in warm water is the best therapy she's ever tried."

"Why, thank you, Ethan," Lelah had replied, a little breathless herself, Cassie had noted. "I…I have done some aquatic therapy and it does help me. But I had to stop when the insurance company refused to pay for any more treatments."

"You'll be able to swim every day at my place." He settled back in his chair, looking pleased with himself.

"How generous of you." She gave Cassie a beseeching look.

"What about Puddles?" Sadie asked.

"Oh, I forgot about Puddles," Lelah said, crestfallen. "I'm afraid we can't leave him alone all day. He…he has accidents. And if we leave him in his kennel all day, he barks and the neighbors complain."

He hadn't missed a beat. Cassie had to give him credit for that, she recalled as she let the dishwater out of the sink. "Bring him along," he'd offered generously. "Just keep him out of the living room." He wrinkled his forehead and gave Lelah one more earth-shattering smile, the backlash of which caught Cassie and stopped her heart for a moment. "White carpet."

"And furniture," Sadie added. "I never go in there."

Ethan shrugged. "I bought the house furnished last winter. I…" He glanced at his daughter. "We haven't had time to change anything yet."

"That will be great!" Sadie said, bouncing in her chair. "I can show you all my Zanies. And my Barbies. And we can all swim together."

"That would be very nice." Lelah had glanced pleadingly in Cassie's direction.

"But—" Cassie had never had a chance to say another word.

"Good," Ethan Hunt had said, the smile coming at her full throttle, but with a hint of an edge to it this time. The smile of a man who had just gotten back a little of his own. "Then it's settled."

CHAPTER FOUR

ETHAN WASN'T QUITE SURE what he'd done by insisting Cassie and her mother—and that darned dog of hers—be in-house babysitters for Sadie. It was kind of like adjusting your race strategy on the fly at Talladega after a crash that shook up the field and left hours of planning scattered across the track. Then you threw out the charts and went with your gut. At the moment, looking down at his daughter, peacefully asleep in the gray light of predawn Tuesday morning, he knew this time at least, he'd made the right call.

Being crew chief of a NASCAR Sprint Cup Series team was a demanding job. He traveled for what amounted to half the year. When he was home in Mooresville he still spent close to sixteen hours a day at the shop. But he wanted Sadie to have one home, not be shuffled around anymore. Cassie Connors being here for Sadie would give him breathing room to find a qualified live-in nanny they both approved of. It was still a daunting task without his mother-in-law's counsel, but maybe Cassie could help him out if he asked her. He was good at judging people, but it always helped to have backup. He'd sensed that same trait in the former Marine. He began to feel a little less intimidated by the coming quest.

He reached down and smoothed his hand over Sadie's hair one more time. She was clutching one of her menagerie of stuffed animals to her heart, a rainbow-striped dinosaur. Rexie, Ethan recalled, having taken pains to learn the names of all of them. She stirred in her sleep and opened one eye. "Daddy?" she whispered. "Is it time to get up?"

"No, doodlebug," he said, bending down to pull the sheet up to her shoulder. "You can sleep in as late as you want this morning."

"Okay," she mumbled. "When I get up I'll ask Cassie if she wants to make breakfast together. Do you think she likes pancakes?"

"Everyone likes pancakes," he said, having absolutely no idea what Cassie did or didn't like for breakfast, but he had a sneaking suspicion it would be whatever his daughter wanted it to be. "I'll see you tonight," he said, straightening.

"Umm," Sadie mumbled and drifted back to sleep. Ethan turned and left the room, leaving the door slightly ajar.

His footsteps echoed along the hardwood hallway and down the wide, curving staircase. The house had four bedrooms upstairs and a master suite downstairs that he used as his office—on the rare occasions when he worked at home. The rest of the first floor consisted of a formal dining room with an imposing antique walnut dining table that seated twelve, and a leaded-glass china cabinet that looked as if it belonged in the White House or someplace equally grand. Across the foyer was the huge, white-decorated living room with its soaring beamed ceiling, mammoth fieldstone fireplace and wall of windows that flanked it on either side.

The view from those windows more than made up for

the house's other shortcomings. Situated at the top of a hill, the house looked out over acres and acres of lush green pastureland and across a small valley to yet another range of low hills dotted with farms and the occasional mini-mansion like his own. The other plus was the kitchen. It stretched across the back of the house with warm cherry floors and cabinets and pale granite counters. He didn't feel as if he had to worry about what kind of mess he or Sadie made when they cooked supper or breakfast together, which like a lot of other things wasn't often enough these days.

Just as he reached the bottom of the steps, the outside motion-sensitive security lights came on, flooding the front walk and the entry in a blaze of light.

He crossed the marble-tiled floor in three long strides and swung open the door. Cassie stood at the base of the three steps that led to the wide, old-fashioned railed porch. She had thrown up a hand to shield her eyes from the harsh light and half turned away as though ready to bolt and run.

He stepped to the control panel and punched in the code to shut off the lights. Immediately they were plunged into the semidarkness of pale, gray dawn. Cassie relaxed her defensive posture, but even from where he was standing he could see she was shaking like a leaf.

He came down the steps and reached out to take her by the arm. "Are you okay?" he asked.

She avoided his hand. "Fine. Fine. Just startled, that's all."

Had he been wrong about her? Was she as nervous and easily frightened as his adopted mother had always been? She seemed so at the moment. "Sorry," he said. "I hate this thing, but the insurance company insists on it out here in the country. At least I figured out how to turn off the alarm bell that used to go off every time the lights came on."

"It startled me, that's all," she repeated. Her face remained white and strained. Her eyes darted from side to side, as though she was searching out hidden dangers in the shadowy corners of the porch where the honeysuckle vines grew thick on their trellises.

"It stays on until daylight. I'll reset it to turn off earlier."

"I'll be ready for it tomorrow," she said, still sounding shaky.

"Sadie's room is right above the porch. I don't want it waking her up every morning when you arrive."

"Would it be better if I used the back entrance?" She was breathing quickly, panting almost, as though she'd run a mile uphill. He narrowed his eyes.

"Are you sure you're okay?"

"I told you I was." She gave one more quick look out across the dark yard before taking a step back as though waiting for him to go inside first. He was all for equality between the sexes, but that was too much for his Southern soul to bear.

"Ladies first," he barked, wincing as she jumped at his brusque tone. Great, now he'd scared her again. This was not the way he'd wanted to start out the morning. "You can use the kitchen entrance if you want to from now on. I always do. It's a lot more convenient to park back there, too."

"I can do that." She walked through the big oak door and stopped in her tracks. Her eyes took in the spacious foyer, the marble floors, the stairway sweeping up into the shadows of the second floor. She tilted her head, her gaze rising three stories to the cupola—or whatever it was called at the top of the house—a low-ceilinged, glass-enclosed space reached by a spiral staircase at the end of the upstairs hallway. "Wow," she said.

"Yeah, I know. A little overdone, but the house has good bones. Would you like a cup of coffee?" he asked. "I have a few minutes before I leave for the shop."

"Shouldn't you show me around the house first? Isn't that what the employer usually does with the hired help the first day?"

That zinger was uncalled for, he decided. He'd been doing his darnedest to make up for the unsettling incident outside the front door. "I thought you might enjoy that more if Sadie showed you around."

"Oh." She had the grace to look sheepish. "Let's start over again, shall we? You have a beautiful home, Mr. Hunt."

"Thank you. And remember, it's Ethan, okay?"

She blinked twice and then nodded. "Ethan." The sound of his name on her lips resonated somewhere deep inside just as her smile had the night before, touching a part of him that hadn't been stimulated in a long, long time. He took an instinctive step back, away from the temptation of asking her to repeat it.

"Let's have that cup of coffee." He started to lead the way to the kitchen when he suddenly remembered she was alone. "Your mother and Puddles, are they waiting in the car?" It was full spring in North Carolina, but the mornings were chilly, especially *this* early in the morning.

She shook her head. "They aren't with me. My mother needs time to get up to speed in the morning. Puddles, too, for that matter. If you don't object I thought Sadie and I could drive back into town later this morning and pick them up."

"No problem at all. I'm sorry I didn't realize your mother's disability was so severe when I suggested she accompany you out here."

"She gets around fine. Just not first thing in the morning, especially not at oh-five-hundred hours."

"None of us do. At least not without a second cup of coffee."

"I haven't even had my first," Cassie confessed. "I nearly overslept."

"I figured you'd be used to getting up at the crack of dawn in the Marines."

"You never get used to getting up at four-thirty in the morning. Never." This time it was her smile that elicited an unexpected reaction from deep inside him, just as intense as when she had spoken his name in that throaty, honey-rich voice of hers.

He smiled back without even having to think about it first. "Then let's get you something to help you face the day."

CASSIE INHALED a deep, lingering breath of the fragrant coffee in the mug she held between her hands. She was still a little shaky from the jolt of adrenaline that had coursed through her body when the security light came on without warning. She hadn't had that kind of reaction for months and months. She'd thought she was over them, but evidently not.

She hoped Ethan hadn't noticed anything more than the fact that she'd been startled. She wasn't ready to explain to him about the PTSD. She wasn't ashamed of her condition or trying to keep it a secret. She just wasn't ready to discuss it with Ethan. But she would have to, and sooner rather than later. It would be dishonest not to. She sighed, wondering yet again why she'd agreed to this whole complicated scheme.

"Did you say something?" Ethan was looking at her over the rim of his mug. The cup he held matched hers, but it was dwarfed by his big hands.

"No, nothing. What will Sadie want for breakfast?" she asked to change the subject.

"Pancakes," he said unhesitatingly. "I hope you don't mind cooking her breakfast. And lunch," he added belatedly.

"No," she said. "I don't mind."

He ran his hand through his short, dark hair. The haircut suited him. It wasn't "high and tight" as the Marines called their signature style. It was just long enough to wave against the nape of his neck and stand up in spikes if he roughed it up enough.

She wondered how it would feel if she ran her fingers through it.

She set the coffee mug down on the tabletop with a bang that made him wince.

"Need a refill?" he asked.

"Sorry." She really had to get hold of herself. She was out of practice in a one-on-one situation like this. She wished she could treat him like a superior officer, unapproachable on a personal level, but he wouldn't stand for that. She'd have to think of some other way to find her balance around him—and soon.

"Hi, Cassie." Sadie was standing in the doorway of the kitchen, a rainbow-striped dinosaur and a pink elephant under her right arm. She was wearing a No. 411 Shelley Green T-shirt and flannel drawstring pants in the same bright purple and green as the colors on the shirt. Shelley, one of the few female NASCAR drivers, drove for Sanford Racing in the NASCAR Nationwide Series. Mia had walked around on clouds for two whole days when she got the chance to work on Shelley's car.

"Good morning, Sadie. You're up early," Cassie said, smiling at the girl's sleep-tousled appearance.

"Something woke me up." She came over to the table and stood close to her father. Ethan put his arm around her waist and gave her a hug. "I thought maybe it was lightning, but I looked out my window and the sun is coming up." A look of relief skittered across Sadie's elfin features. "I don't like thunderstorms," she confessed.

"No storms today," Ethan assured her. "The forecast is clear and sunny. The light went off out front again, doodlebug. I'm sorry. I'll make sure it doesn't happen tomorrow."

"I didn't hear the bell, though," she said. "That's good. Did you set off the alarm, Cassie?"

"I'm afraid I did."

"It's okay. We've been going to look for a new system, but we haven't had time, have we, Dad?"

"Never enough time," he agreed.

"Do you want to go shopping for an alarm system?" she asked Cassie in all seriousness.

Cassie shook her head and smiled. "I think we should leave that up to your dad," she said diplomatically. "But if it's all right with him, we can stop by the mall today. Would you like that?"

"Yes," she said, smiling. "The new Zanies are out. My favorite is a seahorse. I'd like to buy one. I have my allowance," she reminded her father.

"Fine with me. Any shopping expedition I don't have to go on is a good one," he said.

"What about school? Are you on spring break this week?"

"I go to the Wentworth School," Sadie informed Cassie. "This is our spring vacation. I don't have to go back until the first of June."

"The Wentworth School is on a year-round schedule," Ethan explained as he walked to the big cast-iron sink to rinse his coffee mug. "Their philosophy is that children retain more of what they learn if they have a series of shorter breaks during the year, instead of the whole summer off."

"I see," Cassie said. "Do you like your school, Sadie?"

"It's okay. But I'd like to go to school in Mooresville. It's closer."

"I have to get going," Ethan said, ignoring Sadie's declaration.

"Got to get the hauler on the road to Phoenix, right, Dad?"

"Right, doodlebug. Should have left last night, but there was a leak in the brake line. The drivers will have to highball it all the way to Phoenix to be there by Wednesday night."

Phoenix? It took Cassie a moment to remember this week's race was being held at the Arizona track. Ethan would be out of town almost every weekend, she realized. Did he expect her to take care of Sadie then, too? The possibility hadn't been discussed. Not that she had any plans of her own for this weekend, or most others, as far as that was concerned, but she hadn't signed on to be a live-in nanny, only a daily one.

"When are you leaving?" Sadie sat down beside Cassie and arranged her two Zanies before her.

"Thursday morning. Bright and early. Got to get the team settled in before the first practice session."

"I wish I could come along," she said, gazing wistfully at her father.

Ethan patted her on the top of her head as he grabbed a worn black leather bomber jacket from a hook by the back door. "Someday, Sadie, someday. My sister Grace will be looking after Sadie this weekend." He must have seen the question in her eyes. Cassie hadn't realized she was so easy to read. The thought was unsettling, especially considering the source. "Damn, that's something else I didn't explain, right?"

"Right," she said. He was looking agitated himself and that restored her self-confidence—a bit.

"She'll be sleeping over at my sister's at night," he said, "but I'd appreciate it if you would continue to look after her during the day on Thursday and Friday while Grace is working."

"My aunt Grace is a chef. She has her own TV show and everything. I bet you've seen it."

"Is your aunt Grace Winters?"

Sadie nodded proudly. "Her TV show is called *Cooking with Grace*. And she's writing a cookbook, too. It's for NASCAR fans. It's called *The Racing Gourmet*."

"I've seen the show, but I didn't know Grace Winters was your sister."

"She's my adopted sister," he explained, shoving a dark blue Sanford Racing cap, the same blue as his eyes—she noticed unwillingly—on his head. "I'll get you all the landline numbers, and cell-phone numbers and directions to my dad's place and Grace's house—"

"I can do that, Daddy. I have them all in my journal," Sadie said helpfully. "I'm good at keeping track of things," she added for Cassie's benefit.

Cassie gave her a big smile. "So am I. That's what I did in the Marines and that's what I did at my old job."

"Now you're keeping track of me," Sadie said and giggled.

"You're right, I am," Cassie agreed, ignoring a flutter of nerves. They would be fine. Both of them. She could do this. "We might as well get started. I heard you wanted pancakes for breakfast. Want to show me where to find the pancake mix and a bowl?"

"Right over here." Sadie jumped up from the table and padded across the wide-plank floor to a pantry-sized cupboard near the stainless-steel, double-door refrigerator. "You'll have to help me with the bowls. They're too high for me to reach."

"Just point them out." Cassie turned to see Ethan standing with one hand on the doorknob as though he was considering fetching the bowls himself. "Go," she said, making a shooing motion with her hands. "Go get your hauler and your race cars on the road. We'll be just fine."

CHAPTER FIVE

"ETHAN, IT'S GRACE."

He held his cell phone to his right ear and cupped his hand over the left one to filter out some of the noise from the garage floor. He was overseeing the last-minute packing of a few odds and ends that would go with him on the flight to Phoenix in the morning.

"Hey, sis, what can I do for you?"

It was Wednesday evening, and he should have been home two hours ago to have dinner with Sadie. But as usual with this season, nothing had gone according to schedule the entire day. He wanted to be wheels up by seven the next morning for the flight to Phoenix, and thanks to Mia Connors's young legs and enthusiasm, the bits and pieces of equipment and software that had somehow missed being loaded onto the hauler the day before were making their way into a couple of duffel bags to be loaded onto the team plane. Now all he needed was to pack his briefcase and he just might make it home in time to wish Sadie good-night before she went to bed.

"Ethan, I've got some bad news," Grace said. He watched the activity on the garage floor while his stomach sank into his shoes.

"What's wrong?"

"The kids have come down with the stomach flu. It's really bad. I don't know how long I can even stay on the phone. Matthew's vomited twice already and the girls are both looking really green around the gills. I know this is cutting you off at the knees, but I don't think Sadie should be over here this weekend."

"No. No, of course she shouldn't be." He turned and stared at one of the No. 483 car's backup chassis, not seeing the blue-and-gold race car with its emerald lettering, but seeing disaster looming for the upcoming weekend.

"I'm as sorry as I can be, Ethan. I know this puts you in a real bind."

"Don't give it another thought," he said. "You worry about your kids. I just wish I could do something to help you."

"I'm used to this," she said with a sigh. "When one of them gets sick they all get sick. Susan's coming over to help me do the Florence Nightingale thing." She hesitated a moment. "I'm sure Dad would love to have Sadie with him for the weekend." She didn't sound convinced, however.

Ethan wasn't too sure of that, either. His father had retired as the crew chief when his wife was diagnosed with cancer the year before. Now, alone in the big house they'd shared for almost thirty years he was spending more and more time in chat rooms, conversing with what he described as "very nice women," none of whom he'd ever met in person.

"I suppose I could ask him," Ethan said.

"What about the employment agency? Any prospects yet?"

"I haven't heard anything from them for two days."

"Maybe Jared's girlfriend...?" Grace suggested.

"They broke up last month, didn't he tell you?" His brother, Jared, two years younger was a genius with engines. He was employed by FastMax Racing, and Ethan wished he could lure him to the Sanford team to work his magic on the No. 483 car's engines.

"No. I've been so busy we haven't even touched base since the week after Daytona."

"Mom! I'm going to be sick again!" The desperate, tear-filled voice of his nephew resonated through the cell phone.

"Ethan—"

"Go," he ordered Grace. "Take care of Matthew and the girls. I'll get Sadie squared away. Don't worry about us."

"I do worry—"

"Mom!"

"Go."

She broke off the call without saying goodbye.

Ethan snapped his phone shut and slapped it back on the clip on his belt. Great, now what was he supposed to do?

"Ernie said to tell you everything's squared away here for the night," Mia Connors said as she walked rapidly across the garage floor, stopping a few feet from where he stood. Ernie Markham was one of the team's most experienced mechanics, balding, avuncular, approaching sixty, with an eye for spotting mechanical talent and pretty girls—he had a wife, three daughters and eight grand-daughters. He'd taken Mia under his wing her first week in the garage and they were now fast friends. "He also said to tell you we'd be responsible for getting the equipment bags on the flight, so don't worry about them."

"Thanks, Mia." He wondered, briefly, if she had plans for the weekend?

No, he thought. Sadie was just getting used to staying with Cassie. If he was going to beg someone to watch over his daughter 24/7 for the next four days, it would be the former Marine, not her teenage sister.

"CASSIE." SADIE'S VOICE was a whisper. "Puddles is sleeping in my lap." She turned her elfin face in Cassie's direction and the happiness shone from her cornflower-blue eyes. She had Ethan's stubborn tilt to her mouth, and the feminine version of his high cheekbones and strong nose that hinted of Native American ancestry somewhere higher up on the family tree, but she suspected Sadie's blue eyes came from her mother. True, Ethan's eyes were also blue but his were the dark, troubled blue of a stormy sky, not the clear, crystal shade of his daughter's.

"You wore him out playing on the lawn," Cassie said, pitching her voice equally low. Not to keep from waking the napping dog, but her mother. Lelah had fallen asleep on the old-fashioned metal glider with its overstuffed, fern-patterned cushions almost forty minutes earlier. She'd spent the afternoon paddling around in the shallow end of Ethan's luxuriously heated pool, and the unaccustomed exertion had taken its toll.

"Are you ready for your ice cream now?" Cassie asked as Sadie went back to stroking the Yorkie's soft fur.

"I'd like to wait for my dad to come home, if that's okay."

"It's after eight," Cassie said, glancing out the window of the Florida room that butted up to the edge of the pool and overlooked the steeply angled backyard. The spring twilight was fast fading into night, hiding the underbrush and tangle of broken tree limbs that cried out to be landscaped into a rock garden or shady grotto complete with waterfall and curved bridge leading to nowhere in particular.

It wasn't only cooking shows Cassie had become addicted to since she'd lost her job. It was decorating and landscaping shows, as well. She wasn't certain if the interest sprang from a childhood of moving from house to house, never staying in one place long enough to put down roots, literally or figuratively, or if it had manifested itself in the dusty, dry desert setting of Iraq. She felt a smile form on her lips. *Too much introspection here.* Maybe it was simply that she'd like to try her hand at gardening on a larger scale than a few pots along a walkway.

"Do you think Puddles will let me groom him again tomorrow?" Sadie asked hopefully.

"I don't think he'll object. He loves getting brushed almost as much as he likes to play fetch in the yard."

"This is turning out great," Sadie said. "I was afraid my dad would send me to some day care like Grandma and Granddad used to when they wanted to go out for the evening. It's so lame being the oldest kid there. Staying home with you is way more cool."

"This sure looks like a lively bunch," Ethan said from the doorway where he'd evidently been standing for some time. So much for Puddles's skill as a watchdog. He was still snoring gently on Sadie's lap.

"Hi, Dad." Sadie grinned. "I'm glad you're home. I've been waiting for you to have ice cream with me."

Ethan looked worn to the bone, Cassie noticed, and probably the last thing he wanted was a dish of ice cream, but he smiled and said, "I've been thinking of nothing else for the past two hours."

Lelah gave a little snore and awoke from her doze. "Oh, dear," she said. "Did I fall asleep?"

"For a little while," Cassie replied.

"Hello, Ethan," she said, sitting up, patting her hair into place. "How was your day?"

"Hello, Lelah. Busy, very busy," he said, advancing into the room, filling the small space with his presence.

"Would you like something to eat before you have your ice cream?" Cassie asked, rising from her chair so she didn't have to tilt her head so far back to meet his eyes. "We have leftovers."

"We had chicken strips and veggies," Sadie said with a smile. "And fruit for dessert," she added. "Cassie's real big on eating a lot of fruit and veggies."

"I did skip dinner," he replied, looking hopeful.

"I'll fix you a plate while Mom and Sadie bring in the towels from the patio. It's supposed to rain tonight, I think."

"Thanks," he said. "I'd appreciate it. I've got a couple more calls I have to make and I haven't eaten since breakfast."

He reached into his pocket, pulled out his cell and flipped it open. Puddles chose that moment to wake from his nap and take exception to the man in the doorway. With a ferocious growl for a dog who weighed in at six pounds sopping wet, he came off Sadie's lap and bounded across the room, stiff-legged and aching to do battle—or pee on Ethan's pant leg, which was his preferred method of dealing with unwanted visitors.

Cassie sucked in a breath and prepared to make a dive for her pet. Ethan didn't move an inch, just looked down at the excited Yorkie and said, "No, down," in a voice that must have sounded like the Crack of Doom to the little dog.

Puddles sat.

"How did you do that?" Lelah marveled, her eyes big as saucers. "He never obeys me like that."

"Dogs respond best to masculine voices," Ethan said absently. "It's the timbre or something." He looked up from punching in numbers on his phone. "I'm not being sexist," he said seriously. "You can look it up."

Cassie caught her mother's eye and lifted her shoulders in a shrug before following her employer into the kitchen. She headed for the big double-door refrigerator that was nearly empty of food. Ethan and Sadie didn't eat at home much, Cassie had learned from her charge.

"Yes, I'll hold," Ethan was saying as he jackknifed himself into the high-backed, upholstered bench that provided seating on one side of the big pine table. The table held pride of place in the middle of the kitchen floor.

Cassie wondered if two days was too soon to start initiating changes in the Hunt lifestyle. Like going grocery shopping, instead of bringing things from home to tempt Sadie's fussy appetite. She didn't mind the expense. Ethan was paying her very well, but it wasn't right to open the doors of a huge restaurant-size refrigerator like this one and find it almost showroom empty.

"You'll let all the cold air out standing there with the door open," Ethan said from behind her.

"Sorry." She whirled around with a guilty start. "It won't happen again."

"It was a joke," he said. "Didn't your mom tell you that every time she caught you looking inside a fridge?"

Cassie gave a little snort of embarrassed laughter. "Yes, she did. But right now I'm staring into the refrigerator because it's empty and I was hoping if I wished hard enough it would fill up with food," she said, only half teasing.

"What?"

"You need to go grocery shopping," she said, opening the door wider so he could see the bare interior. He stared at her blankly, the cell phone still held to his ear. "To buy food for your daughter," she explained. "And her nanny. Her nanny's mother. And their dog," she added with a grin.

"Oh, God," he said. "I forgot. I'm sorry. You've been feeding her out of your own pocket, haven't you?" His face flamed with embarrassment. "How much do I owe you for the food?"

"Nothing. She eats like a bird." That had worried Cassie and Lelah. They'd been at pains to tempt Sadie with whatever sounded good to her and had been rewarded with a decided improvement in her appetite when chicken strips and raw veggies and dip had been substituted for broiled skinless breasts and steamed carrots, one of the half-dozen or so frozen dinners Lelah had found sitting forlornly on a shelf in the freezer of the mammoth side-by-side.

"I'll get some food delivered," he said, staring down at the display on his phone, obviously wondering if his call had been dropped.

"Delivered? You order your groceries and have them delivered?" Cassie had never heard of such a thing.

"There's a service in Charlotte. They deal mostly in frozen food. But they'll bring fruits and vegetables if you request them." He looked at her. "I don't usually order them. They spoil." He paused a moment. "We eat out a lot."

"So Sadie tells me. I'm just learning what she likes. I can tell you what she doesn't like, though." She picked up one of the frozen entrées. "Salmon with mango chutney and mushroom risotto."

"It's a gourmet service," he said apologetically, and Cassie smiled. She couldn't help it.

"Why don't I take Sadie grocery shopping tomorrow? It will be fun."

"I'd appreciate that. The problem is we won't be here tomorrow. I'm going to have to take Sadie to Phoenix with me."

The scrabbling of toenails on the bare wood floor heralded the approach of Puddles and Sadie. "What? Awesome! We're going to the race in Phoenix?" Sadie's voice rose to a squeal. "You've never taken me to a race before." She danced across the kitchen, around the corner of the table to stand behind Ethan. She threw her arms around his neck and laid her head on his shoulder. "Oh, Daddy, I can't wait to go!" It was the first time Cassie had seen Sadie so animated and demonstrative toward her father. She felt a little kick in the chest as she remembered back to when she was little and her father was the center of her world. Before he showed his true colors and left them all to fend for themselves.

Ethan sat very still for a moment, then closed his phone on his waiting call. He lifted his hand and covered Sadie's with his own. "Do you really want to go, doodle-bug?" he asked.

"Yes, oh, yes! But I thought I was going to stay with Aunt Grace."

"Your cousins have the stomach flu. You can't go there this weekend, so I made arrangements for a motor home for the two of us." The worried frown was back, but thankfully Sadie couldn't see it from where she was standing.

"Wow! Do we get to fly on the team plane?"

"Yes," he said. He caught Cassie's eye and she thought she saw a flicker of true panic flare deep in the blue. "We leave first thing in the morning." His next words took Cassie completely by surprise. "I know you only signed on for a forty-hour week, but I'm hoping you'd like to come with us—and your mother and Puddles, too," he added with what sounded like desperation in his voice.

Cassie opened her mouth to indeed remind him that she had only been hired to watch over his daughter during the normal business hours, but after only a couple of days on the job, she'd already learned there was no such thing as normal business hours for a man who was a crew chief for a NASCAR team.

"Please. I really need your help," he added softly in a slow drawl that sent prickles of sensation up and down her spine and derailed her indignation before it could get up a real head of steam.

"Oh, Cassie, say yes!" Sadie exclaimed. "Please say yes. It will be a blast. A real blast!" She danced back the way she had come and slipped her arms around Cassie's waist.

Ethan looked like a man at the end of his tether with nowhere else to turn. In the Marines you were always there for your buddy. But Ethan wasn't her buddy. He was her boss and she should make a stand, on principle if for no other reason, but once her arms closed around Sadie's slender form, once she felt the girl trembling with excitement and delight, there was nothing else she could do but say, "Yes, of course we'll come."

CHAPTER SIX

"I NEVER REALIZED how cold it could be in the desert," Lelah said as she made her way carefully down the steps of the motor home Ethan had arranged for the three of them—and Puddles—in one of the reserved lots at the speedway complex. She moved one of the canvas chairs from its place beneath the retractable awning that ran the length of the forty-foot unit and lifted her face to the morning sun. "Mmm, that feels good."

"You'll be glad for the shade later in the day," Cassie warned. "It's going to get close to ninety."

"Yes, but it's a *dry* heat," Lelah said. "Not like back home. This is the life, Cassie," she said, wriggling into her seat as she gazed longingly at the big motor home. "I'm going to get me one of these outfits when I win the lottery. We'll hire a driver and go traveling all over the country."

The unit they were staying in was an older model, its paint job slightly faded from the intense Arizona sun, but inside everything was polished and well maintained. It lacked the high-end glitz of the million-dollar motor homes Cassie had seen showcased on TV, but it was far nicer than anything the Connors women could afford.

"Have you seen my bed?" Lelah asked her. "Who would

ever have imagined the bed in an RV would be as comfortable as mine at home is?"

"I don't think they refer to these babies as RVs," Cassie told her, heading back inside to grab two mugs of coffee she'd brewed earlier. "It's a motor home. We're way beyond RV-ing here."

"It doesn't matter what you call it. I want one. Remind me to buy a lottery ticket first thing when we get back home. We'll share and share alike when we win."

"It's a deal." Cassie turned around and lifted Puddles down the steps to do his business in a small patch of scrub behind the motor home. Sadie was in the shower and they were alone for a few minutes. They hadn't met their neighbors on either side, but from the team stickers and driver's pennants displayed in the windows and on flagpoles attached to the sides of the vehicles, Cassie suspected they were fans and not employees or family of the race teams.

Ethan was staying in another motor home, with a couple of bachelor members of his team, somewhat closer to the track than the lot where they were parked. He'd helped them settle and then disappeared. He'd kept his word about the groceries, though. The motor home was well stocked with food. Cassie smiled to herself. She was already learning that if Sadie's father made a mistake, he corrected it ASAP. She had no idea how the three of them would be able to eat all that food before the weekend was over. Sadie had already talked her into baking triple-fudge brownies before the day heated up so they could have them later topped with hot fudge sundaes. She was going to leave here looking like a blimp.

"Hello," a voice called out. She turned her head to see

an elderly woman, her silvery hair twisted into a roll on top of her head, bracelets jangling from her wrists and rings on every finger, making her way purposely toward the motor home in a four-seater golf cart.

"Hello," Cassie said, rising to her feet.

"Hello," Lelah echoed from her chair.

"I'm Juliana Grosso," the woman said, exiting the cart and holding out her hand. "I heard you were here, so I dropped by to say hello."

"I'm Cassie Connors, Sadie Hunt's nanny. And this is my mother, Lelah."

"How nice of you to welcome us," Lelah said, indicating an empty chair beside her. "Are you a friend of Ethan and Sadie's?"

"I know Ethan's father, Dan, very well. He and my husband have been friends for years. I also knew his mother, Linda, a very nice woman, may she rest in peace. My grandson and my great-grandson are both NASCAR Sprint Cup drivers," Juliana said with a proud smile as she seated herself beside Lelah. "And my new great-grandson-in-law, too."

"Oh, of course." Lelah colored prettily. "How silly of me. Your grandson is Dean Grosso. He's the current champion, isn't he?"

"Yes, he is. Although he retired and isn't defending his title."

"And your great-grandson is Kent Grosso. He was last year's champion, correct? And Dean's daughter, Sophia, married Justin Murphy last weekend. He drives the Turn-Rite Tools car." Lelah'd taken to reading everything she could find on the Internet about NASCAR, cramming as though she might be asked to write some kind of exam.

Juliana laughed and clapped her hands. "Goodness, yes. That's right."

Cassie grinned and gave her mother a thumbs-up. "Way to go, Mom. Mia will be proud of you." Her sister had not been invited to come to Phoenix. Rookie mechanics didn't travel with the team. She'd taken the news that Cassie and Lelah were going to make the trip philosophically. Ernie had promised her she could work on next week's car setup, and that was more than ample compensation in her eyes.

"My younger daughter works for Sanford Racing," Lelah said proudly as Juliana took a seat beside her. "She just graduated from NASCAR Technical Institute. She wants to make a career in NASCAR."

"I hope she achieves her goal," Juliana said. "We need more women in the sport."

"Dean's wife, Patsy, is a car owner, isn't she?"

"Why, yes she is." Juliana looked pleased that Lelah knew that fact. "She and Dean bought Cargill Racing from Alan Cargill just before his death last winter."

"That poor man. I remember hearing about his murder on TV and reading about it in the papers. What a terrible thing to have happen," Lelah sympathized. "They haven't caught whoever killed him yet, have they?"

"No. I'm afraid not." Sadness clouded Juliana's expressive face and dimmed her eyes. For a moment she looked much older than she had first appeared. "I'm afraid the killer might never be caught."

The Grosso family was no stranger to sadness, Cassie recalled. There was also the story of Dean and Patsy

Grosso's kidnapped baby, Gina, taken from her hospital crib, lost for thirty years and long believed dead. But lately NASCAR Nation had been abuzz with rumors that the baby hadn't died but was now a grown woman with ties to the sport. Speculation was rife as to who she might be— at least according to Mia, and now Lelah, who were avidly following the blogs and chat rooms where speculation flourished. "Could we offer you a cup of coffee?" Cassie asked to lead the conversation on to less upsetting subjects.

"No, thank you," Juliana said, standing up. "I must be on my way. I just wanted to invite y'all, and Ethan, naturally, to a little cocktail party Milo and I are having tonight. We don't usually travel to races anymore, so we thought we'd have a party."

"Why, thank you." Cassie felt a little out of her depth. She wasn't exactly a servant, but she also wasn't comfortable accepting invitations for Ethan and his daughter.

"It's all very casual. You and Lelah and Sadie are very welcome even without Ethan. The man's allergic to parties, I swear, always has been a loner. We've known him forever, Milo and I. Milo's my husband," she explained belatedly. "He gave Ethan his first job back when Grosso Racing still fielded a NASCAR Sprint Cup team. He was just out of high school and green as grass." She waved one hand in the air, bracelets jingling and catching sparkles of sunlight. "That's a story for another time." She stood up, giving Cassie a long, assessing once-over, her eyes lingering momentarily on the small globe-and-anchor tattoo just above her ankle that she'd gotten on her first leave after boot camp years before. Juliana's eyebrows rose slightly, then she chuckled. "You just pass on the invitation and tell him I'll be mighty put out if he doesn't do the gentlemanly thing and escort you ladies to the party."

"I'll tell him," Cassie said. "But I can't guarantee he'll come."

"You're a Marine," Juliana said, pointing to the tattoo. Cassie noted she didn't say ex-Marine. She nodded. Juliana chuckled approvingly. "My oldest brother was a Marine, God rest his soul. I know the breed. You'll make sure he's there."

"IT'S NOT AN INVITATION," Ethan grumbled. "It's a royal summons." He had stopped by the motor home on his way to the track to ready the car for Trey's qualifying run tomorrow. But first he wanted to check on Sadie. And, face it, he admitted to himself, he wanted to see Cassie. He couldn't seem to get her completely out of his thoughts at any time during the day or night. He didn't know which was worse, being distracted at the garage or in his dreams.

The dreams, of course. He hadn't had sexy dreams like those…well, in years and years.

"I got that impression."

"She seemed very nice." Lelah was sitting just outside the awning that ran the length of the motor home, soaking in the sun. She was wearing a Greenstone Garden Centers cap and a pair of the reflective sunglasses Trey Sanford endorsed. She looked ten years younger than when they had first met only four days earlier. Four days? Was that all it had been? He never would have guessed these women could have become so much a part of his life and Sadie's in so short a time, but that was exactly what was happening.

"Miss Juliana's going to have ice cream for dessert," Sadie said. "And something called tiramisu. And brownies.

Now we can save ours for tomorrow." She beamed. She was wearing a Sanford Racing cap, a twin to his own, a junior-size pair of Trey's shades perched on the brim. Adam must have seen to it that the promotional items had been stocked in the motor home, and he made a mental note to thank his boss for the gesture. A tube of heavy-duty sunscreen resided on the table beside her game station, and Ethan felt himself relax another notch when he realized that Cassie had already taken steps to ensure Sadie's fair skin was pro-tected from the sun.

"We can't miss out on food like that now, can we?"

"No way," Sadie said, rolling her eyes heavenward and rubbing her tummy.

Puddles stood up, stretched and ambled out from under Sadie's chair where he'd been dozing. He made a beeline for Ethan and began sniffing at his shoe. "Don't even think about it," Ethan said. Puddles sat back on his haunches and hung his head.

Sadie jumped up from her seat and scooped him into her arms. "I think he needs to pee. Can I take him behind the motor home, Cassie?"

"Sure."

Sadie grabbed a leash from the table, snapped it onto the dog's collar and disappeared around the end of the motor home.

"That dog minds you better than he does the rest of us put together." A smile tilted the corners of Cassie's mobile mouth as though she was remembering something amusing. He felt a strong urge to demand she tell him what the joke was. She was wearing denim pants that came halfway down her calf and a tank top in a pale lemony yellow that made her skin glow like honey in the diffused light beneath the canopy. Her hair was brushed smooth today, pushed back behind her ears and held in place with yet another pair of Trey's signature sunglasses.

"Juliana Grosso was gracious enough to invite all of us for the evening," Cassie informed him. She was sitting on the steps of the motor home, her arms wrapped around her knees. "I hope you don't mind."

"Mind? Why should I mind?" he muttered. "Juliana's parties are famous and not so frequent anymore. She cooks like an angel. My sister Grace is one of her biggest fans."

"I'm so looking forward to it," Lelah said.

Ethan wished he was. The last thing he wanted was to have to make small talk with half the drivers and crew chiefs on the tour when he had so much on his mind. Trey still wasn't happy with the car's setup and he was having trouble pinning down just what was wrong. It was his job to interpret his driver's wants and needs, but so far this season he was doing a damned poor job of it.

"Are you sure it won't be awkward having the hired help attend a party of your friends and peers?" Cassie asked in that challenging way of hers.

He snorted, jerked back into the moment at hand by her remark. "You sure have some screwed-up ideas," he said. "We're not living in some kind of gothic novel, here."

She looked a little surprised at his candor, but didn't respond in kind. She just gave a brief nod and said, "Okay. I promise not to act like the governess showing up at the ball uninvited. I guess I'm just nervous about hobnobbing with the elite."

He snorted again and rolled his eyes. She hitched up

her shoulders and said, "Okay, I won't mention it again. Will Sadie be the only child there?" she asked. "She'll probably want to take her game station if that's the case. Will that be okay?"

"She can take it if she wants to, but I imagine there'll be other kids there. Juliana casts a wide net when she entertains and a lot of the drivers and crew chiefs, and even the owners, travel with their families in tow these days. Some tracks even provide day care and all kinds of activities for the older kids."

"Perhaps we should look into Sadie attending. Is that allowed?"

He frowned a moment. "I'll have to see about getting her credentialed. All three of you, I guess. That is, if you'd like to get onto the track."

"I'm sure Sadie would be thrilled." Cassie looked pretty thrilled herself, but he could tell she was trying hard to keep it from showing on her face. "I don't think my mother is ready for the whole track experience just yet."

"Then she's probably better off watching everything on TV. Sadie can't go into the garage area in any case. No one under eighteen is allowed inside—NASCAR rules. But just about anywhere else is okay these days."

Cassie raised one eyebrow slightly. "Really?"

"Yes, really. Family-oriented and equal opportunity. And I'm right in the vanguard of change," he reminded her, getting in one more zinger. "I hired your sister, remember?"

"You've got me there," she replied, and before she turned away to go back into the motor home he thought he saw her smile again.

CHAPTER SEVEN

MUSIC PLAYED from a small acoustic system positioned in a window of Dean and Patsy Grosso's motor home. Tables, laden with everything from barbecue and nachos to lasagna and Juliana's world-famous tiramisu, to hot dogs and hamburgers and platters of fresh fruit and ice cream sundaes for the kids, ranged along one side of a tentlike awning that had been erected between the reigning NASCAR Sprint Cup Series champion's motor home and Milo and Juliana's.

Flanking the motor homes were two more luxurious diesel units, the more elaborate belonging to Kent and Tanya Grosso, the other to newlyweds Justin and Sophia Murphy. By parking the inner motor homes to the far left and right of their appointed spaces, the Grosso/Murphy clan had created a small courtyard, which was now crowded with several-dozen adults and quite a few children.

As he'd told Cassie earlier, Juliana—known to everyone in NASCAR as Nana—truly did cast a wide net when she put on a party. There were more than a couple of owners, eight or ten drivers and their girlfriends and wives and children, a scattering of crew chiefs and hungry pit crew members still in team uniforms taking a break from garage and hauler duties. All eating and drinking and enjoying the cool of the desert evening.

Ethan finished off the plate of Southwest-style barbecue and baked beans and took a long swallow of his beer. He hadn't expected to enjoy himself this much. He hadn't expected to enjoy himself at all, if truth be told, but there was something about a good meal and a few drinks among friends that had a way of easing away the strain of a long, frustrating day.

Trey Sanford had started it off by taking exception to the setup Ethan had chosen for the car. Trey had stormed out of the garage as soon as he could unstrap himself from the car seat, and Ethan hadn't seen him since. He knew his hotheaded driver would calm down sooner or later and apologize, be ready to sit down and talk strategy, but the younger man's erratic behavior over the past couple of weeks was beginning to wear down Ethan's patience and cause uneasiness among the team.

Ethan had a suspicion that the latest round of media attention on Trey's frequent late-night trips to Mexico might be at the bottom of his driver's bad moods. That and the fact that he and Becky Peters had called it quits again, this time for good, it seemed.

The romance was another victim of the elaborate facade of evasions and half truths that Adam and Trey had constructed to hide the real reason behind Trey's forays south of the border. Better, in Ethan's opinion, to get the truth out in the open and get past it, not play these elaborate games with the media. But he was only the crew chief, not the team owner, so Adam called the shots and Ethan did as he was told. It wasn't his secret to tell.

"Dad, is it all right if I go to Jamie and Dana's motor home and watch a movie? Their mother said it was all right. She said they would bring me home in their golf cart when it was over." Sadie stood before him, flanked by two other girls about her own age, her face a study in suppressed excitement. He'd been so preoccupied he hadn't even seen her walk up to him. He forced his dark thoughts into the back of his mind and took her hands in both his.

"Slow down," he said, grinning. "Aren't you having a good time here?"

"Yes, but I really, really want to see the movie."

Ethan switched his attention to the other little girls. "You're Shakey Paulson's daughters, right?" he asked. Shakey was a good guy, a journeyman driver for Fulcrum Motorsports who was just about the same age as Ethan. He had two teenage sons and two daughters—the girls standing before him—and had been married to his high-school sweetheart for almost twenty years. He and Laura used to spend quite a bit of time with the Paulsons when they were all first married.

"Hey, Ethan, good to see you here." It was Shakey's wife, Coral, swooping up from behind him in a cloud of expensive perfume to wrap her arms around his neck and give him a kiss on the cheek. "It's been way too long."

He tried to rise from his seat to greet her properly, but she pushed him back down. "Don't get up. I just wanted to second the girls' invitation to have Sadie over for a movie and popcorn."

"Popcorn? I just saw you and Cassie going by with a hot fudge sundae," he said to Sadie. "How can you be hungry again already?"

"We are," his daughter assured him solemnly. "Aren't we?" She swiveled her head from left to right to urge her new friends to back her up.

The Paulson girls nodded in enthusiastic agreement. "Starved," they agreed.

Coral laughed. "You're all going to grow up to look just like me," she lamented, gazing ruefully down at her rounded hips and generous bustline. "A moment on the lips, forever on the hips, Grandmama always says."

"We're starving," the youngest—Dana, Ethan recalled—insisted. "Honest."

"Well, then, I guess I need to get you home and feed you. We really would love to have Sadie come, too, Ethan. I'll see she's home by ten."

"Thank you for inviting her. We need to check in with Cassie, though," he said to Sadie. "Let her know what's going on."

"She's over there talking to that guy," Sadie said, half turning to point Cassie out in the crowd around the buffet table.

"Cassie Connors is Sadie's companion," Ethan explained to Coral. "She's helping out while Sadie's grandparents are on a cruise."

"The blond Marine?"

"Yes." Ethan willed himself not to look too long in Cassie's direction so Coral wouldn't notice his interest in her.

It really wasn't even necessary to look her way. Cassie's image was already seared in his brain as though someone had used a branding iron on him. She was wearing a sundress in a cool mint-green color that just skimmed the tops of her ankles and clung to her curves in a less-thannannylike way. Her hair was pulled up on top of her head in a kind of wild and, he had to confess, wildly sexy tangle held precariously in place by the tortoiseshell combs he'd seen her wear before. A thin gold chain graced her neck and tiny gold balls dangled from her earlobes. She looked cool and confident, and when she smiled, as she did right then—at Rafael O'Bryan, damn it—she almost took his breath away.

"How did you know she's an ex-Marine?" he asked, proud that his befuddlement didn't come through in his voice.

Coral punched him in the arm. "There's no such thing as an ex-Marine. Keep that in mind. Shakey picked her out of the crowd right away. It's some kind of radar they all have, I think."

"That's right. I forgot Shakey was in the corps."

"Four years," she said proudly. "And she has a globe-and-anchor tattoo on her ankle. Don't tell me you're too old to have noticed her ankles."

"She wears pants most of the time," he said, hoping his face hadn't turned red.

"You're getting old, Ethan," Coral said, giving him a playful punch on the arm.

"Daddy, please. May I go?" Sadie interrupted, growing impatient.

"Go check with Cassie."

"Okay, come on, you guys." The trio hurried off.

"She's the spitting image of her mother," Coral said, her voice softer, filled with nostalgia.

"She does look a lot like Laura." A tiny familiar pang of sorrow nipped his heart, but it had mellowed over the years and no longer caused him much pain.

He watched as Sadie and Cassie came toward them, clasped hands swinging, Sadie laughing up into Cassie's smiling face. The Paulson girls had veered off to say goodbye to their father, wrapping their arms around him in exuberant hugs as though they were leaving for a round-the-world trip and not just walking a hundred yards to their motor home.

"I think you made a great choice in a nanny for Sadie. She needs someone young and vibrant in her life," Coral said under her breath.

"I'm beginning to think the same thing," he replied, unable to stop a smile from spreading across his face.

Coral gave him a long, considering look. "I think Sadie's not the only one who's going to benefit from this association. Introduce me, won't you, please?"

SADIE LOOKED out the window of the Paulson motor home at the orange-and-pink sunset fading to purple above the hills behind the racetrack. "Wow," she said, leaning her elbows on the back of the sofa, Jamie Paulson on one side of her, Dana on the other, doing the same thing. "That's something, isn't it? All those brown hills and wild colors. I've never been to the desert before. It isn't as hot as I thought it would be, but it's sure way different from where we live." She liked saying that. *Where we live.* It made her think that maybe she would be able to stay friends with these guys when they all got back to Mooresville. Most of the girls that went to the Wentworth School lived in Concord, too far away to visit without making a big production of getting there and back.

"That's because you've never been here in the summer,"

Jamie informed her loftily. She was twelve already and thought she knew everything. "It's hot enough to fry eggs on top of your car."

"You've done that?"

"No," she confessed, coming down a peg. "But that's what my granddaddy says and he does live here. Well, in Tucson, anyway. That's why we got to come along this week. We're on spring break and our grandmama and granddad Paulson live there."

"Do you travel to a lot of races?" Sadie asked, following her new friends' example, turning away from the desert sunset to dip into the bowl of buttered popcorn Mrs. Paulson had helped them microwave before she went back to the Grossos' party.

"In the summer we do," Dana said, punching buttons on the TV remote to mute the "Coming Attractions" part of the DVD as she munched away on her popcorn. "Not Talladega, though."

"Or Michigan," Jamie added. "Mom and Dad say the infields are kind of rowdy there. Too many parties."

"Are you going to go to school in Mooresville when you're in junior high?" Dana asked, eyeing the bright pink nail polish on her toes. Sadie had already figured out that Dana liked to do girl things more than Jamie. Jamie was kind of a tomboy. Sadie liked to do girly things, but she liked sports, too.

"My grandmother wants me to go to the boarding school my mother went to. I want to go to regular school, though. I hope my dad will let me."

"I bet he would if you asked him," Dana said. "It shouldn't be up to your grandparents to choose your school."

"My mom died when I was really little, so I spend a lot of time with my grandparents when my dad's working. They really love me and I love them, but I don't want to go to boarding school."

"Well, you've got a whole year to get them to let you transfer to regular school," Jamie said practically. "If they love you as much as you say they do, they'll probably let you. Do you miss your mom?" she asked, changing the subject.

Sadie nodded, not quite trusting her voice, picturing the photograph of her mom holding her when she was a little baby that she kept on the table beside her bed. She looked like her and had her smile, Grandma always said. "I miss her all the time, but it's okay. I know she's in heaven watching over me and my dad. And now I have Cassie to do things with and be my friend." She was too old to have a nanny and Cassie had said she didn't like being called one, either, so they had agreed to be friends. She smiled, feeling better again. "She's going to watch the race with me."

"Don't forget your earplugs," Jamie said, making a face.

"I've already got a pair, and a headset, a big padded one with a radio inside so I can listen to my dad talk to Trey in his car," Sadie told them proudly. "And credentials and everything." She was finally going to get to see her dad do his work. No more watching races on TV, hoping to catch a glimpse of him when they showed pit stops and stuff. She couldn't wait to see him in his dark-blue-and-gold uniform on top of the big toolbox where he watched the race and talked to Trey over the radio. And if Trey won she might even get to go to Victory Lane. And it was all because of Cassie saying she would come along to watch over her.

Watch over her. She liked the sound of that. She

wished that Cassie could always be there to watch over her, like a mom.

Like a mom. The thought sent tingles up and down her back, then darted into her heart and sent out warm feelings all through her body. Why hadn't she thought of that before? Cassie was young and pretty and a lot of fun to be around. Maybe if she wished very hard, her dad might start thinking the same thing.

And then, just like in the movies, maybe they would fall in love.

"EXCUSE ME," Cassie murmured, smiling apologetically into the dark eyes of the tall, olive-complexioned man in the orange-and-brown team uniform deep in conversation with Ethan. "I need to have a word with Mr. Hunt." The party was beginning to wind down, people drifting away in twos and threes to their motor homes, but a dozen or so guests were still gathered beneath the awning enjoying the cool of the desert evening.

Ethan turned to her and a smile creased his face. Cassie's heart rate doubled instantly. "What is it, Cassie?"

"I have a request from Sadie," she said. "I think she was a little worried that you might say no if she asked you directly."

"Wade Abraham, this is Cassie Connors, my daughter's nanny," Ethan said by way of introduction.

"Sadie's *friend,*" Cassie corrected with a grin, holding out her hand to the man whose dark good looks testified to his Middle Eastern heritage. "Sadie is too old for a nanny, or so she informs me. We've settled on 'friend.' It's nice to meet you."

"You, too," he said with a smile that revealed strong white teeth. "Welcome to the wonderful world of NASCAR."

"Thank you. Everyone's been very nice."

"What is it Sadie's afraid to ask me?" Ethan inquired.

"She called me on my cell a few minutes ago. She wants to know if she can sleep over at the Paulsons' motor home," she said smiling. "Evidently she and the Paulson girls are now BFF and can't stand the thought of being separated."

"BFF?"

"I know that one," Wade stated. "Best friends forever."

"Exactly." Still smiling, Cassie turned to Ethan. "Coral says she's happy to have her, if you approve."

"I suppose it's all right," he said. "Did anyone bother to ask Shakey what he thought about three giggling preteens camped out in the salon of his motor home when he's driving in the NASCAR Nationwide race tomorrow?"

"I wasn't privy to that conversation," Cassie replied diplomatically. "I'll arrange to pick up Sadie after breakfast. It seems waffles are on the menu for tomorrow morning."

"I could go for that," Wade said, grinning.

"Me, too," Ethan agreed.

"I have one more favor to ask," Cassie said, not quite able to call Ethan by his first name in front of this stranger. She couldn't explain why, except she was afraid that with the way her heart was still hammering—the aftereffect of that smile—it might come out sounding far too breathless and intimate. "My mother is getting tired. Could I borrow your golf cart to take her back to the motor home?"

"Your mother is here, too?" Wade asked, lifting one dark brow.

"Yes," Cassie said, "she is."

"And her dog," Ethan added dryly.

"Ah, I see, Sadie's acquired an entourage."

"I guess you could say that. You're part of the Turn-Rite Tools team, am I correct?"

"Wade is Justin Murphy's car chief. He's also married to Kim Murphy, Justin's cousin," Ethan explained.

"I went to high school with Sophia," Cassie remarked.

Sophia Murphy, radiantly happy and evidently as determined a hostess as her formidable great-grandmother, had greeted her warmly when she first arrived at the party. Cassie had been surprised to find Sophia remembered her from high school a decade earlier. "You joined the Marines right after graduation, didn't you?" she'd said. "I was in awe of you doing that. I would never have been able to make the grade," she'd confessed with a dazzling smile that Cassie remembered well. "Come," she'd said, linking her hand through Cassie's arm. "I want you to meet my parents. And my great-grandfather, Milo. And my husband...." She'd giggled. "Oh heck, I'll just introduce you to everyone." From that moment on Cassie and Lelah and Sadie had been enfolded into the Grosso family circle and made to feel as welcome as old, dear friends come to visit after a long absence.

"Sophia, like her mother and great-grandmother, is a force of nature," Wade said.

"NASCAR's like a family business, isn't it?" Cassie said, thinking of the intertwining of families and teams and relationships that in some cases stretched back generations.

"Or a medieval guild. Passing trade secrets on from father to son."

"That, too," she said, laughing.

"Dan Hunt was one of the best crew chiefs in the sport. He taught me just about everything I know about stock car racing when I broke into the NASCAR Sprint Cup Series. Is he ready to climb back up on the war wagon yet, Ethan?"

"Dad's beginning to get antsy sitting at home. He's lonely without my mother, but he hasn't definitely said he's ready to come back."

"It'll be a lucky team that gets him when he does." Wade held out his hand again. "It was nice meeting you, Cassie. If you'll excuse me I have to be going. Kim stayed home for this race and I want to call her before it gets too late back there."

"How's she doing?" Ethan asked.

"Great. The kidney's functioning perfectly. She's back to work full-time. We're even starting to talk about having a family." He turned toward Cassie and explained, "My wife had a kidney transplant last year. It was touch-and-go for a while, but she's fine now."

"Good to hear," Ethan said, and sounded as if he meant it. "Take it easy, Wade. And good racing."

"Same to you, buddy."

"Nice guy," Cassie said as Wade moved out of earshot. "Now if you'll just point out your cart—"

"I'll run you and your mother back to the motor home," Ethan said in his usual forceful manner. "I've got a few things I need to check up on in the hauler before I call it a night. I'll drop you off on the way there."

"All right." She would have liked a look at the hauler, the epicenter of Sanford Racing's brain trust at the track, but she didn't have the nerve to ask for a tour. "I'll go get her." Two minutes later she was back with Lelah. Her mother was wearing a lightweight cotton sweater in a brilliant peacock blue over her favorite black sheath. She looked younger and prettier than Cassie could remember seeing her for a long time, but fatigue still dulled the brightness of her eyes. Cassie hurried to put a steadying hand under her elbow when she stumbled a little on the uneven ground.

"Goodness, I only had a single glass of wine, but I feel as tipsy as if I'd drunk the whole bottle," she confessed as they waited for Ethan to maneuver the cart into position to pick them up.

"Don't overdo the alcohol, Mom," Cassie cautioned automatically. "You don't want to trigger a flare-up."

"I only had a single glass," Lelah reassured her. "It's just that I can't remember having so much fun. So many nice people to talk to and all their stories about NASCAR are so interesting. Did you know Juliana's husband was an FBI agent years ago? He actually met J. Edgar Hoover. Imagine that."

Cassie had spent a few minutes in conversation with the Grosso patriarch. Although past ninety, Milo Grosso was as sharp as a blade. "He's a very interesting man."

"And such a gentleman." Lelah looked over her shoulder, her face wistful. "I wish Mia could be with us," she whispered as Ethan backed close to where they were standing.

"Mia's getting her wish, too, Mom," Cassie reminded her. "She's right where she wants to be, working in a NASCAR Sprint Cup garage."

"Yes and we have Ethan to thank for that, too."

Ethan unfolded himself from beneath the golf cart's low canopy and came around to where they were standing. "Your carriage awaits, ladies," he said with a sweep of his hand.

"Thank you, kind sir." Lelah laid her hand in his and he closed his fingers very gently over hers, putting his hand beneath her elbow to assist her onto the seat.

"Ready, Cassie?" he asked, turning the full force of his smile on her. She was glad he wasn't wearing his team uniform like Wade Abraham and some of the other men at the party had been, because it made his eyes seem even bluer, his shoulders broader. She would probably have melted in a puddle at his feet. He was sexy enough in a dark sports jacket and open-throated shirt.

Hurriedly Cassie stepped up onto the back seat of the cart before he could offer her his hand as he had her mother. If he touched her he would feel her trembling—and she didn't want that, didn't want him to know how strongly he affected her.

She was shaking like a leaf, not from nerves or an incipient panic attack, but because of that damned smile. It made her feel all weak and wobbly inside, giddy and breathless and vulnerable—far too vulnerable for her own good.

CHAPTER EIGHT

"WOULD YOU LIKE to ride over to the hauler with me?" Ethan asked as he slowed the golf cart to a halt outside the door of the rented motor home. He hadn't intended to prolong his time with Cassie this evening, but the words just seemed to jump onto his tongue and out of his mouth as though they had a mind of their own.

"I don't have any credentials," Cassie reminded him, exiting the back seat and moving to her mother's side before he could offer Lelah his assistance.

"You do now." He reached into the small storage compartment in the dashboard of the cart and pulled out three plastic cases with NASCAR lanyards already affixed. "I picked these up earlier for all three of you," he said, handing Lelah her pass and giving Cassie the other two, her own and Sadie's. "I didn't have time to give them to you earlier."

"Thank you," Lelah said. "I was wondering how I would be able to visit Juliana tomorrow without one of these. She invited me for tea."

"I'll arrange for someone to drop off a cart for the three of you. It's too far to walk from here to the owners' and drivers' lot."

"I appreciate the kindness." Before turning to mount the

steps, Lelah gave him a long, considering look that reminded him uncomfortably of her daughter's. "I won't wait up," she said, closing the door behind her.

"I won't be late," Cassie promised. He glanced down as she slid onto the passenger seat beside him and spied the small tattoo on her ankle. The one Coral had mentioned earlier, a globe and anchor, the U.S. Marine Corps emblem. He'd never in his life expected to find that particular tattoo sexy, but he sure as hell did tonight. He should have kept his eyes on the road, it turned out.

From that moment on he became acutely aware of every move she made, every breath she took. He could feel the warmth of her skin through the thin fabric of her dress where her thigh almost touched his. He could smell her perfume whenever he inhaled. Her perfume and something else, the soft, sweet scent of a woman. A woman to hold in his arms, to make love to and to lie wrapped together with after. How long had it been for him? A couple of years, maybe longer. He had mourned Laura for a long time, and when he did begin to date again, the relationships had been temporary and superficial. He'd never found a woman he'd cared for enough to offer her a place in his life or Sadie's.

But this week, out of a clear blue sky, he'd allowed Cassie to come into their lives in a far more intimate way than any other woman he'd known.

"Did you enjoy the party?" he asked, searching for something to talk about that would divert his thoughts from the dangerous direction they were taking.

"Yes, very much, and Sadie was thrilled to meet the Paulson girls. I don't think she had any idea there would be kids her age here this weekend."

"In the summer there will be more. A lot of NASCAR people travel with their families these days." He braked to a halt to let the uniformed security guard at the gate inspect their credentials and allow them into the infield tunnel. "I'm sorry I couldn't get you a space in the owners' and drivers' lot this weekend—not enough notice."

"We're happy where we are. Do you know there's a grocery store set up in the motor home lot? A big one. I couldn't believe it. No wonder all the tailgating parties have such great-looking food. We're going on a shopping expedition tomorrow although I don't know where we'd put any more food if we did buy something. This place is huge," she said as she looked around her. "I had no idea."

"Is this your first time at a NASCAR track?" He had himself back under control now. He let himself relax just enough to enjoy her company, but not enough to wonder how it would feel to run his fingers through her wildly curling hair.

"Yes, even though I've lived near Charlotte all my life."

She sounded as impressed as Sadie probably would be tomorrow when she came through these gates. He grinned, just thinking about it. He was going to break off early and watch the NASCAR Nationwide Series race with them from seats on the hillside just like any other fan, something he hadn't done in years. "Things are pretty tame right now. Tomorrow at this time the place will be packed with people for the NASCAR Nationwide race. Saturday evening will be an even bigger crowd for the NASCAR Sprint Cup race."

Cassie watched the garage stalls pass with interest, taking in the array of brightly painted cars, some covered with tarps for the night, others gleaming beneath the light.

But when they began to trundle past the team haulers, she peered from beneath the cart's canopy as if she'd never seen anything like them before in her life. And she probably hadn't, forty-three titanic eighteen-wheelers parked in laser-straight rows. The colorful paint schemes, each one as elaborate as the cars they represented, were mostly hidden in the gathering desert night, but still impressive. The interiors of the trailers were bisected by narrow walkways flanked by stainless-steel counters and floor-to-ceiling storage bins. Hydraulic tailgates, used to raise and lower the race cars stored in overhead spaces, were lifted to shelter team members waiting for their rides to area hotels where they stayed during race weekends. Team members who were at this moment giving Cassie subtle glances and evidently liking what they saw, judging from the swinging heads and grinning faces.

He pulled up to the No. 483 car's hauler, deserted except for Pete Swenson, the driver and part-time spotter for Trey Sanford. The short, heavyset man, who'd once been a commercial long-haul driver, turned off the industrial vacuum he was using to sweep the debris from the thick rubber mats laid down under the lift gate to form a kind of temporary patio.

"Hey, Ethan, whatya doing back here this late?"

"Hi, Pete. I forgot the fuel-consumption charts," he responded, exiting from the cramped confines of the golf cart.

Pete glanced at his watch after touching his finger to the brim of his ball cap and smiling politely in Cassie's direction. "Ten minutes till I have to lock her up."

"I'll be back in five. The garages and haulers are locked down every night," Ethan explained to Cassie. "Nobody in or out until seven tomorrow morning—NASCAR rules. If there was more time I'd give you a tour of the hauler tonight, but it will have to wait until tomorrow."

"Tomorrow will be fine."

From the corner of his eye Ethan caught a couple over-the-wall guys from Rafael O'Bryan's team taking notice of her, and on the other side, Hart Hampton's car chief, just recently divorced, was also checking her out.

If he hurried he could be back in three minutes.

"Better tell Adam and Trey time's getting short," Pete drawled, his accent attesting to a childhood spent in the deepest reaches of the South.

"They're here?"

"Been in the lounge for the past twenty minutes or so." "Lounge" was a misleading name for the small, cramped space at the front of the trailer that served as dining area, meeting room and team headquarters when they were on the circuit. He wondered what his team owner and driver were doing in the hauler this time of night as he walked toward the sound of voices coming through the partially open door.

"Are you okay? Why another trip down there so soon?" he heard Adam Sanford ask.

"I'm fine. Strictly follow-up."

"The press is getting curious, Trey. Be careful. If they get wind of another trip so soon—"

"They'll think I've got another beautiful señorita under my spell," Trey said in a voice filled with a mixture of anger and disgust. "Besides, my breaking up with Becky will give them all enough to write about for the rest of the weekend."

"I'm sorry about that."

"Don't be. We were never serious enough to make it, anyway."

"It might have helped if you'd told her the truth about all these trips to Mexico, instead of—" Adam's voice fell silent abruptly. "Someone's coming."

Ethan had made no attempt to hide his approach. He paused to rap on the doorframe. "Adam? Trey? It's Ethan. Mind if I come in?"

The door opened, fully revealing his boss's tall, imposing figure. "Sure, Ethan, come on in."

"I came to get the fuel-consumption charts. I want to go over them one more time," he said, stepping into the small space. Trey was sitting at the console that held a couple of computer monitors and printers. He rose when Ethan entered the room and picked up his driving helmet, settling it under his arm, unconsciously striking the pose that graced his sponsor's advertising posters.

"They're right here," Trey said. "I was looking them over. I didn't get a chance earlier." He stabbed at the printout with his finger. "The setup you used today makes sense with these numbers. Sorry I went off on you."

"We'll do fine qualifying tomorrow," Ethan said, accepting the sheaf of computer paper and the apology. "It's a good car. The track should come to us once the sun goes behind the hills and the temperature drops. If not we'll think of something else."

"You'll think of something else. I just drive the car, remember."

"You'd be better off paying less attention to what the media's saying and more to your crew chief," Adam said tersely, his eyes locked with his brother's. Trey was shorter and slighter than either Adam or Ethan, who both topped six feet, and younger by several years.

"I'd be happy as hell to stay out of the media's way. That just isn't going to happen." Trey hadn't been tempered by the same fires as his brother, who had taken over the family race team at an early age after their father's untimely death. When Trey won the NASCAR Nationwide Series championship the year before, the decision had been made to put him in the NASCAR Sprint Cup Series car. The torch had been passed to a new generation of the dynasty, and it was now Ethan's duty as much as Adam's to make sure Trey carried on a proud racing family's winning tradition.

And to keep the family secrets.

"I made a few notes on the charts," Trey continued. "Don't know if they'll mess you up or not. I'll print out a clean copy, if you give me a minute."

"No problem, I'm interested in what you have to say." Ethan took the printouts from Trey's hand. "Team meeting's at eight," he reminded him.

Trey gave his brother a quick glance. "Can't make it at eight," he said.

"Trey's doctor wants another follow-up." Adam's gaze was clear and direct but gave away nothing of what was going on inside his first-class brain.

Ethan switched his attention to Trey. "No new problem, is there?"

"I'm fine," Trey said impatiently. "There was a screw-up with the last scan. The implant's working fine, but the doctor won't sign off on it without a redo. You know NASCAR won't let me race without her signature on the paper."

Ethan nodded. When he had become Trey's crew chief, he'd also become privy to information that no one outside the Sanford family was aware of.

"We'll make it nine-thirty, then. Will that give you enough time to get back here?"

"I'll be there. All signed, sealed and NASCAR-certified fit." Trey brushed past Ethan and stalked out of the hauler.

"Thanks for cutting him some slack." Adam reached for a leather jacket he'd draped over a chair.

"Did I have any choice?" Ethan asked him.

"Look, Ethan." Adam shrugged into his jacket. "I know you don't approve of the way Trey's handling this whole business, but you know what a hit we could take if this gets away from us. I know we're running out of time. Just hang in with me. I'll figure out some way to keep this from blowing up in our faces."

"As your friend, you know I'll do as you ask. As your crew chief, I have to tell you Trey's head isn't in the game. He's distracted and he's losing focus."

"Just stay with him a little while longer, Ethan. You can get him back on track. I know you can. You've got enough focus and drive for ten men. That's why I hired you."

"I can't drive the car for him."

"I know that."

Ethan wrestled with his conscience for a moment longer. "I'll do as you ask. But if he doesn't come around soon he's getting taken out of the car. Lack of focus can be costly. I won't have him out there on the track if I think he's a danger to himself or others. Understood?"

For a moment Adam looked as if he was going to tell Ethan to go to hell. Ethan half expected it. Instead, Adam gave a short, sharp nod. "Understood," he said. "You do what's best for the team."

"I intend to. For the team. And for your brother."

"WELL, WHAT HAVE we here?"

Cassie swiveled her head to find herself confronted by a very handsome man about her own age. She didn't need the blue-and-gold racing uniform, the high-tech helmet tucked beneath his arm, or the million-megawatt smile that accompanied the greeting to alert her to his identity. This was Trey Sanford, the driver of the No. 483 Greenstone Garden Centers car. His likeness stared out of an almost life-size poster taped to Sadie's bedroom wall, where it was the first thing she saw when she opened her eyes in the morning, the last thing she saw when she turned off the light at night.

Cassie suspected her charge kept the poster so prominently displayed not because of this handsome creature but because of another figure in the background of the artwork. He was wearing the same blue-and-gold uniform, arms folded across his broad chest, face set in stern, uncompromising lines, his gaze focused off in the distance, and he seemed to be standing guard over the younger man and the car. Like Sadie it was that second figure that riveted her gaze each time she saw it. Ethan Hunt, the car's crew chief, the man who called the shots and kept the focus for this handsome, willful-looking boy.

"I'm a 'who,' not a 'what,'" Cassie said, withholding her own smile.

"Sorry," he said, not looking a bit chagrined, although now that she was paying attention she noticed that the devil-may-care smile somehow didn't quite reach his brown eyes. "I'll try again. Who have we here?"

"Cassie Connors," she said. "Who are you?" Although she knew perfectly well who he was.

Trey Sanford laughed, going along with the joke. "I'm

the defending NASCAR Nationwide Series champion," he said. "I drive the No. 483 Greenstone Garden Centers NASCAR Sprint Cup Series car."

"Sorry, still don't have a clue." Two could play at this flirting game. She was beginning to enjoy herself.

"I'm on the cover of *Racing Insider* this week."

"I've never seen the publication," Cassie said primly.

"They call me NASCAR's most eligible bachelor," he said, still keeping up the joke.

"I'm not looking for a husband. I've heard they're more trouble than they're worth." Pete, the man Ethan had spoken to earlier, snorted in laughter as he folded up a camp chair and stowed it in a compartment beneath the big truck.

Trey ignored the jab and gave the Sanford Racing cart a quick glance. "You're here with Ethan?" The inflection in his voice alerted her to the fact that Ethan bringing a woman to the team hauler was something that didn't happen often.

"I'm his daughter's companion," she said, mindful of her promise to Sadie not to say she was her nanny.

"Sadie's a cute kid. She's been hanging around the garage a lot these past couple weeks."

"She won't be there anymore. She'll be staying home with me."

"Sounds like fun," he said, resting his foot on the cart's running board, his helmet balanced on his knee. It was a darned sexy pose and Cassie wasn't entirely immune to his charms, although she tried hard to be. He leaned slightly closer. "If you need any help riding herd on her, you can call me. I'm always up for a good time."

Too close. He'd passed the line into her private space.

She stiffened momentarily. "From what I've heard, your idea of a good time wouldn't be suitable for an eleven-year-old," she said, not funning at all.

He suddenly seemed to tire of the game. "Let's start over," he suggested. He stuck out his hand. "Hi, I'm Trey Sanford."

She let him fold her hand in his. "I'm still Cassie Connors."

"Welcome to NASCAR and Sanford Racing."

"Thank you."

Ethan loomed up behind the shorter, slighter man. He glanced over Trey's shoulder and scowled. Cassie realized Trey was still holding her hand. She felt a small flush of heat color her cheeks. "You can let go of my hand now," she said.

"Do I have to?" Trey sighed theatrically, holding on tightly enough she had to tug to disengage their hands.

"You do," Ethan said gruffly, stalking around the cart to take his seat beside Cassie. "Pete's locking the hauler."

Trey glanced at his watch, big as a teacup and filled with dials, the kind astronauts and airline pilots advertised in glossy magazines. Ethan's had a lot of bells and whistles, too, she'd noticed, but it was nowhere near as ostentatious as Trey's. "I've got to be on my way. I'll be seeing you around the track," he said to Cassie.

"I doubt it," Ethan announced before she could reply. "Cassie's got better things to do with her time."

They drove in silence for a few minutes, passing other carts and people on foot, all of them wearing the credentials and lanyards that Cassie was already beginning to realize set her a little bit apart from outsiders to the sport. "Sorry," Ethan said as they waited to be passed through the outer gate to the access road that led to the motor home parking lots. "I shouldn't have said that."

"No," Cassie agreed, "you shouldn't have. I know what my duties are. I won't neglect Sadie."

He turned his head to give her a sharp look. "That's not what I meant by it."

"I know that, too," she responded, looking straight ahead. She didn't want to discuss Trey Sanford's attentions. "I won't be spending my time mooning over your driver, either, if that's what you're worried about."

"Your private life is none of my business."

"You're right, it isn't. But my behavior when I'm with Sadie is, so your concern is appropriate and has been duly noted." She meant to add that Trey wasn't her type, NASCAR hotshot or not, but since that might goad Ethan into asking what her type was, she kept her mouth shut, letting him think she didn't answer because they'd halted to let yet another security guard check their credentials.

"Heard your driver's ordered up a helicopter to take him to the airport," the man said with a leering grin that grated on Cassie's nerve endings. He gave their credentials a cursory glance. "Must be another one of those late-night flights to see his lady friend in Mexico, huh?"

Ethan didn't say a word, but from the tense line of his jaw and shoulders, Cassie deduced he wanted to. He retrieved the passes and handed hers over without a glance, still ignoring the security guard, who finally realized he'd crossed a line he shouldn't have and opened the gate, waving them through with a half salute.

"Damn," Ethan said under his breath as they glided

along under a desert sky bright with stars. "This whole thing is getting out of control."

Cassie half turned in her seat so that she could watch his face. His hands were tight on the small steering wheel and his expression was grim. "I see other drivers' names in the news all the time. Why should Trey Sanford be any different? What's so terrible about him having a girlfriend in Mexico?"

"It's not the girlfriend in Mexico," he said finally. "It's something more serious and a lot more complicated than him jet-setting around." He stopped short, realizing he might have said too much. "Look, forget I said that, will you?"

"Of course," she said. "It's none of my business." She faced straight ahead again, surprised by how much it hurt to have him dismiss her so quickly.

"It isn't," he said, and the pain in her chest deepened. "It's team business and I should have kept it to myself." He brought the cart to a halt in front of the motor home where, through the partially open blinds, she could see her mother, sitting on the sofa watching television.

"I understand," she said, horrified by the tiny catch she heard in her voice. She was a Marine, for heaven's sake. A combat veteran. Why on earth was she getting all choked up because this man she barely knew didn't trust her with his private business and said so?

He scooted around in the seat until his knee nearly touched her thigh. The motor homes on either side of them were quiet, their owners either sleeping or away for the evening. "No, you don't," he said. "NASCAR is big business these days and an even bigger newsmaker. You don't have any experience with the media, do you?"

She shook her head, not trusting her voice. "No," she finally managed. She didn't want to look at him, but her pride wouldn't let her turn away. "Why don't you explain it to me," she said, "so I know what to expect."

He touched the case that held her new credentials, her new passport into his world. He didn't touch her bare skin, but he might as well have, as a rush of warmth spread all the way through her body from the top of her head to the soles of her feet. "This marks you as fair game," he said. "Once they see you with me, or Trey, or any other recognizable face in the sport you'll be on their radar."

"I won't let them near Sadie," she said fiercely.

Surprisingly, he chuckled. "I have no fear of that, Sgt. Connors," he said, his voice deep and soft, almost a caress. "And to be honest," he admitted in a far less intimate tone, "I don't know of any of them who'd try to get to me through a child. But be careful. Don't talk to them. Not on the phone. Not in person. If any one of them, print or television, electronic, paparazzi, whatever medium, corners you here at the track, just say 'No comment' and send them to me."

"Yes, sir," she said, relaxing a bit. He wasn't angry with her. Her heart rate picked up a few beats. He was looking out for her. *He was trying to protect her.* And Sadie most of all, she reminded herself sternly.

"I don't want you to walk into an ambush," he said.

Everything inside her went cold. "Don't worry," she said grimly. "I won't."

WHAT A JACKASS he was. Ethan rolled onto his back, trying to ignore the snoring from the two men sleeping in the main cabin of the motor home. He folded his hands behind his head and stared at the light patterns on the ceiling. Why had he made that stupid remark about keeping her from walking into an ambush? He couldn't have picked a worse cliché if he'd thought about it for weeks.

The look of horror on her face had wrenched his heart even if it had lasted only a moment. She had been wounded in combat and many of the injuries suffered by military personnel were caused by ambushes. He had imagined her bleeding and broken beside a burning vehicle, and the shock of it struck him dumb. He couldn't find a single word to say to her to make it right. Before he could pull himself together Puddles had jumped onto the back of the sofa and began barking, getting himself tangled up in the blinds. Cassie had mumbled good-night and hurried up the steps to help Lelah extricate the annoying animal. Any chance he had to apologize evaporated like rain on the desert. He didn't know when he'd find another chance to be private enough to make amends.

Another hammer blow of emotion struck him in the chest. He wanted to be alone with her. Not with his daughter or her mother or even her dog in tow.

Alone. Just the two of them.

Odds were good that it wouldn't be anytime soon, though.

CHAPTER NINE

"CASSIE. IT'S SO LOUD!" Sadie was wearing a grin that almost split her face in two. Her eyes were so wide open Cassie could see white all around the crystal-blue irises. "I can't hear myself talk." She clapped her hands over the huge, padded earphones that contained a race scanner and walkie-talkie combination so they could talk to each other without removing them.

"Here." Cassie reached over and adjusted Sadie's headphones, cushioning her ears. "Better?" she mouthed. They were alone on the grassy hillside above the racetrack that was open for general-admission seating, a unique feature of the Arizona racetrack. There had been a problem with Trey's car, and Ethan had begged off accompanying them at the last moment.

"Thanks." Sadie turned back to the racing, zeroing in on Shelley Green's car, watching Sanford Racing's NASCAR Nationwide Series female driver circle the track, holding her own against the rest of the field.

She felt a tap on her shoulder. The cars had cycled to the far side of the mile-and-a-half oval, and she could almost hear herself think. "She's good," a male voice said as she lifted the earphones from her head, letting them rest against her neck. Despite the protection, her ears were ringing slightly as she lifted her gaze to a familiar wide smile on a mouth that was made to kiss.

"Hi, Trey," Sadie said, giving the NASCAR Sprint Cup Series driver a short wave.

"Hi, doodle." Sanford Racing's team members had all picked up on Ethan's nickname for his daughter, and she seemed to enjoy the sense of belonging it gave her when they used it.

"And hello to you, Miss Cassie." He touched his finger to the bill of his cap. The worn and faded headgear sported a number and a color combination she didn't recognize immediately.

"Hi yourself," she mouthed back. Not the wittiest retort, but it was too noisy for snappy conversation, anyway. "What are you doing here?"

"Looking for you."

Looking for her? Cassie was glad she was sitting down, otherwise she might have fallen. "Whatever for?" she wondered aloud.

He laughed. "Why not? Your mom said you were watching the race from up here, so here I am, too."

He'd been to the motor home looking for her? He hadn't just stumbled across them on an incognito trip among his fans? Cassie hoped the amazement she felt at the revelation didn't show on her face.

Trey pointed off in the distance to where the string of race cars was a colorful, fast-moving blur. "Shelley's good enough to drive in the Show full-time. I hope she gets her shot. As long as she doesn't take my ride," he added, a self-mocking twist to his grin. "Enjoying yourself?" he asked, placing the headphones that had been dangling from his long, tanned fingers over his ears as the cars came roaring back down the track toward them.

Cassie nodded and gave him a thumbs-up as she replaced her own headset. Trey Sanford's sudden appearance was slightly unnerving—and something of a letdown, owing to the fact that when she'd first caught sight of the male silhouette out of the corner of her eye, she'd found herself hoping it belonged to Ethan.

"Mind if I join you for a couple of laps?" he asked as the field roared by once more. They were sitting on folding chairs beneath a plastic awning. There were no grandstand seats, so people brought lawn chairs and coolers and sat on blankets on the ground to watch the race. Whole families were picnicking above and below them, and children ran here and there among the spectators as the early-evening shadows lengthened over the racetrack. It had been a gorgeous, sunny afternoon and the desert sunset promised to be just as beautiful.

Just the kind of sunset to watch with a sexy man at your side. Unfortunately, just as with the grin and the kissable mouth, this was the wrong sexy man.

"Sure," she said. "Have a seat."

Trey hunkered down on the balls of his feet between their chairs. "How do you like the race so far?"

"Great. We're both thrilled Shelley Green's doing so well." Shelley was in ninth place and had just made a great pass on a slower car. Sadie had been beside herself with excitement.

"Damn, I wouldn't be surprised if that kid hasn't inherited her dad's racing genes," Trey remarked, watching as

Ethan's daughter followed the action on the track with rapt attention. "Before you know it ol' Ethan will have her on the box beside him with a stopwatch keeping lap times."

"She's very quick." And motivated, Cassie thought. Sadie would take up rocket science if she thought it would please her father.

It was too noisy to indulge in long conversational gambits, and Cassie figured Trey would soon move on. NASCAR Sprint Cup drivers didn't often hang out in public areas of the racetrack with the fans; even Cassie knew that. And the reason they didn't hang out in the public areas was that they caused riots and stampedes of fans and media types when they did show up. Even as the thought went through her mind, people began to pick up on Trey's presence among them.

"You're causing a stir," she said as the cars raced for the far turn, fading sunlight glinting off their windshields. "I don't want Sadie caught up in a stampede," she warned him.

He looked around. "Rats," he said. "I figured no one would spot me up here. They all think I'm out chasing beautiful women all around the northern hemisphere." He wouldn't have to run very fast to catch them. Wearing a vintage Hawaiian shirt and khaki shorts and the sexy wrap-around sunglasses he was never photographed without, he looked like sex and sin all wrapped up in one neat package.

"Instead, you're sitting here in the cheap seats with us."

"Jeez, I didn't mean—" The roar of forty-three racing V-8s drowned out the rest of his apology. Dark color rose beneath his tan.

Cassie laughed—she couldn't help herself. It was the most human she'd seen him look or act. "It's okay. I know what you meant and Sadie's too young to be offended by a male-chauvinist-pig remark like that one."

He grinned sheepishly. "Let me make it up to you. How about dinner tonight?" He looked around, noting a couple of brave fans making their way closer to check to see if it was really Trey Sanford. "Hurry," he demanded. "Say yes. I have to go."

"No," she said, instead. "Thanks, but no."

"Why not?"

"I'm here to take care of Sadie, not add notches to your belt," she said bluntly. "Thanks for asking, though."

"You're a hard woman, Cassie Connors." He glanced over his shoulder at the advancing fans. "Damn, too late for a fast getaway."

"What?" Cassie had been distracted by his asking her out. It had never entered her head that he would. She had seen Becky Peters at Juliana and Milo's party, tall, willowy, drop-dead gorgeous. Short, curvy, with a pair of combat boots in the bottom of her closet didn't translate to his type at all.

Cassie took a moment to look around, and her breath caught in her throat. There were people everywhere—at least it seemed that way to her—holding out programs and hats, asking Trey to autograph the clothes they were wearing, some even presenting their bare arms if they had nothing else for him to sign.

"Cassie, what's going on?" Sadie asked. Cassie turned her head to see more people crowding in on Sadie's chair. She stood up hurriedly, holding out her hand to the child.

"Come on, Sadie. We have to get out of here." The suddenness of the onslaught of fans had caught her by surprise.

They were completely surrounded now. Trey had risen gracefully to his feet and attempted to back off a few feet to move the crowd away from where they were sitting, but there were still far too many people pressing around them.

Cassie felt her heart rate rev up, and her breath began to come in quick pants. Trey lunged forward and snatched her hat off her head, scrawling his name across the bill with a marker one of his fans must have given him. "Here you go, ma'am," he said, still smiling, but only with his mouth. She couldn't see his eyes, hidden behind his dark glasses, but she could feel the tension radiating from him. "I've got to be moving on."

He handed her the hat. She took it automatically and glanced down. He'd placed a set of cart keys inside. Her cue to leave, too? She shoved it back on her head, the keys still inside. She helped Sadie to her feet and the two of them began to work their way out of the crowd. The people closest to them parted ranks without a fuss, seeing that Cassie had her autograph and was only moving out of their way. Further back she wasn't so lucky. Two excited women refused to give up the ground they'd staked out.

Cassie swiveled to outflank them and lost hold of Sadie's hand. Panic erupted full-blown and paralyzing. Suddenly she couldn't move, couldn't draw breath to call out for Sadie to come to her, couldn't see her through the red haze of fear that obscured her vision. She stood rooted to the spot for what seemed half a lifetime but could only have been a handful of seconds. Then she felt a small hand grasp her shirttail and Sadie was at her side once more.

"This is scary," Sadie said, her eyes apprehensive.

"We're going right now." The effort to speak the words

in a calm and rational voice nearly drained Cassie's last reserves. She was operating on instinct alone as she pushed past the outer fringe of excited fans and broke free into the desert twilight. The lead pack of cars came roaring out of the turn a hundred feet away. The noise was deafening. Cassie wanted to scream with terror, but she clenched her jaw and kept on walking, focused on her objective—the gate in the fence.

"What about our stuff?" Sadie panted when the cars had passed and the noise of their engines was muted enough to let them speak again. Cassie broke into a jog, pulling Sadie along with her as she labored to outdistance a threat she could no longer see, only feel.

"Later." The single word was all she could manage. Her legs were beginning to feel like jelly. Her chest hurt from the effort to draw air into her lungs. She wanted nothing more than to find some safe place to go to ground and pull Sadie in with her to keep her safe. There was a sudden squeal of brakes, followed instantaneously by a loud bang as a car hit the retaining wall. Cassie fought to keep a scream from breaking free of her constricted throat. A plume of smoke and dust rose heavenward from the far side of the track. A roar went up from the stands. People on the hillside jumped to their feet and began pointing and raising binoculars to their eyes to get a better look. The decibel level from the orbiting cars dropped significantly as they slowed their headlong pace. Sadie jerked Cassie to a halt.

"There's been a wreck," she said, pointing.

"Don't stop. Keep moving."

Sadie stared at her, round-eyed. "Are you okay?" she asked.

A figure loomed up beside them. Cassie flinched, but then recognized Trey's face through the fog of panic that still gripped her in iron claws.

"Something's happened on the backstretch," Trey said. "It distracted everyone enough I managed to get away. They're right behind me, though. We've got to keep moving."

Cassie nodded. It was all the acknowledgment she could manage.

"This way," Trey said. He reached for her hand and led them off toward the gate Cassie had been making for.

The guard stationed there saw them coming and swung the gate wide. "I told you it wasn't a good idea to go up there without some backup, Trey," he said.

"Next time I'll take your advice, Mack. Thanks for your help." He pointed out a golf cart and they all scrambled into the front seat. Cassie was operating on sheer instinct by this point. She could barely understand what Trey was saying to her. Didn't realize he was asking for the ignition keys until he plucked her cap off her head and pulled them out of the inner lining. "Let's get out of here," he said.

They zoomed along the access road toward the lot where Cassie's rented motor home was parked. Cassie kept Sadie's hand clasped between her own, afraid to let go, and tried to bring her breathing under control. They were out of danger, she knew that much. She had nothing to fear on Sadie's behalf any longer, but her heart still hammered in her chest and anxiety still arced along her nerve endings. The scars on her leg burned with the same fire that seared her lungs. She rubbed her leg convulsively.

"Cassie's shaking like a leaf," Sadie said. "What's

wrong, Cassie? Are you sick? Did you get hurt running away from those people?"

Cassie shook her head, not trusting her voice. She was afraid that if she tried to speak she'd break into tears.

Sadie looked past her to Trey. "Do you have your cell phone?" she demanded. Cassie barely registered what she was saying. The urge to crawl into a hole, into her bed, somewhere, anywhere warm and dark, and fall asleep was almost overwhelming.

"Yes."

"Please call my dad," she said, squeezing Cassie's hand so hard it broke through the fog of panic like a tiny ray of sunlight and let her focus for a moment on what was going on around her. She squeezed back. "Tell him something is wrong with Cassie and he has to come to the motor home to help us. Right now."

"WHERE IS SHE? What's going on?" Ethan had just been leaving the hauler when his cell rang and he'd heard Trey's voice, tense with strain, issuing an order for him to get over to Sadie's motor home, ASAP.

The only details he could get from his driver were that Sadie was fine. The problem had something to do with Cassie and an incident on the hillside. "Damn," he muttered under his breath. "I shouldn't have sent them up there alone."

He didn't take the time to ask how Trey had become involved in whatever had happened. That explanation could come later. He didn't bother with one of the team's slower, smaller electric golf carts, but hailed a guard passing by in one of the gasoline-powered golf carts that track security used. Five minutes later he was standing in the salon of the motor home.

Trey was seated at the built-in dining banquet, drumming his fingers on the tabletop. Sadie was heating water on the stove, a tin can of teabags resting alongside a mug and a spoon on the counter. Cassie was nowhere to be seen, but the pocket door that separated the salon and kitchen from the bath and bedroom was firmly closed and he could hear water running in the shower.

"Daddy!" Sadie launched herself across the salon and into his arms. "We got mobbed by Trey's fans up on the hillside. They were everywhere. Cassie…Cassie must have gotten really scared. She…she's not acting like herself. I'm worried about her."

"Where is she?"

"In the shower. I'm making her a cup of tea," Sadie said proudly. "I know that will make her feel better. Do you think she might want some cinnamon toast to go with it? I'm good at making toast."

"Sure, doodlebug. Toast is good. Where's Cassie's mother?"

"Lelah got invited to watch the race with Juliana Grosso in her motor home," Sadie said. "Should we call her to come home?"

"Let's wait a little, okay? Go ahead and make Cassie some toast. Trey, what the hell happened here?" His heart was still hammering in his chest, but everything seemed to be under control for the moment and he began to relax.

"Sadie told you most of it. I didn't count on getting recognized up there. I just stopped by to say hi to Cassie and Sadie."

"What the hell do you mean you didn't think you'd be recognized? Your picture's plastered all over the Internet and the sports channels."

Trey's hands fisted, then relaxed. "Yeah, well. Another stupid move on my part. Add it to my list of sins, all right?"

"What happened to Cassie?"

"I'm not sure. If I had to take a guess, I'd say she had some kind of panic attack." Trey shrugged. "She was as cool as a cucumber while we were stuck in the middle of the scrum. Took the cart keys I passed her and hustled Sadie out of the crowd without a backward glance. I caught up to them a couple of minutes later and we made a beeline for the cart and headed here. That's when it happened. She just sort of went to pieces for a couple of minutes after it was all over. Sat there white as a sheet, shaking like a leaf, staring off into some kind of world of her own. One filled with nightmares and monsters," he added under his breath so that Sadie wouldn't hear.

"A panic attack? Are you sure that's what it was?" He recalled the look of terror that had flitted across her expressive features that first morning when the security light coming on overhead had startled her so much. Had she been on the verge of such an attack then? If she had, she hid it very well.

Trey shrugged again. "I'm not a doctor or a shrink, but that's what it looked like to me."

The pocket door slid open and Cassie emerged with her hair wrapped in a towel, Puddles following protectively at her heels. She was wearing a pair of loose drawstring pants, black, made of some sort of silky material that clung to her legs and hips, with a faded red T-shirt with USMC in equally faded gold lettering across the front. She'd pulled a long-sleeved cotton sweater over the T-shirt.

She was white as a sheet and her eyes were dark with pain and stress, but she managed a genuine smile for Sadie when his daughter presented her with a cup of weak tea and two pieces of toast slathered with butter and a thick sprinkling of cinnamon sugar, Sadie's favorite. "Thank you, Sadie. This is exactly what I need."

She took the mug of tea in both hands. She was still trembling, Ethan noted, as the tea came close to sloshing over the edge of the cup. She turned the heartbreakingly brave smile on Trey. "Thanks for getting us back here. I couldn't have done it on my own."

"Hey, I had to rescue you. It was my fault you got caught up in that mêlée in the first place."

She took a sip of her tea as though to moisten her throat. Even so her next words were barely audible, but her gaze was as unswerving as always. "You're right, Ethan. I did have a panic attack. I had hoped it wouldn't happen again, but that doesn't excuse the fact that I didn't inform you of my condition when you hired me."

He opened his mouth to respond, but Trey beat him to it. "Look, since you're feeling better, I'll get out of here and let you discuss this in private." He whisked the ever-present dark glasses out of his pocket and held them between his hands. "I really am sorry, Cassie. I wouldn't have put you and Sadie in danger for all the money in the world. I promise you nothing like that will ever happen again."

"There's no way you could have stopped it," she said. "It's forgotten."

"I appreciate that. One more thing before I go," he said.

"Yes?"

"I'm not taking your 'no' as a final answer. Be prepared for me to ask you to dinner again."

"Trey—"

"Fair warning, that's all I'm saying." He turned to Ethan. "I'll tell the guard outside everything's okay in here. Send him on his way."

"Thanks."

The door opened and closed behind him. Ethan turned around. Cassie and Sadie were seated together on one side of the banquet. Sadie was holding Puddles on her lap, and Cassie was dutifully chewing and swallowing a piece of toast, washing each bite down with a swallow of tea. He slid onto the bench seat across from them. "Are you sure you're okay? We could head over to the Infield Care Center and get you checked out." The racetrack provided a full-time medical staff during race week available to team and family members, as well as ailing fans. The staff also provided emergency treatment for drivers during the race.

"I don't need to see a doctor," she said sharply. "The worst is over."

"Should I send for your mother?"

"No," she said sharply. "No, let her finish watching the race."

"It scared me when you got upset," Sadie said, burying her face in the dog's topknot. He was wearing that damned camouflage bow again today. It was the most ridiculous thing Ethan had ever seen on a dog—except for the fact it suited the little Yorkie to a T.

Cassie put down her mug and gathered Sadie and

Puddles into a hug. "I'm so sorry, doodlebug. That's the last thing I wanted to have happen."

It was the first time he'd heard Cassie use his late wife's pet name for their daughter, and the feeling it engendered was bittersweet, comprised of equal parts sorrow for what was lost and a longing for what might be.

"Why were you so afraid?" Sadie asked. "I didn't like being crowded by all those people, but I wasn't that scared." She snuggled against Cassie's shoulder, patting her arm with one small hand.

"I don't understand it completely myself," Cassie said quietly. "It started when I came back from Iraq. It happens to soldiers sometimes when they've been hurt…or…seen bad things. It's called post-traumatic stress disorder. I have it." She looked across the table at Ethan, her hazel eyes filled with regret. "I thought I was better. It's been a long time since I've had an attack that severe. Forgive me. I wasn't keeping my condition from you intentionally. There just hasn't seemed to be a good time to tell you yet. Everything's happened so fast this week. And, well, to be truthful, I hoped there wouldn't be any episodes like today. I was overly optimistic, I guess."

"Are you going to get better?" Sadie asked barely above a whisper. "Will they go away forever someday?"

"I hope so."

"We'll help you, won't we, Dad?" his daughter said with all the confidence of the very young and untested. "We'll be there for you if it happens again."

Cassie laid her cheek against Sadie's hair for a moment. He could see her struggling to keep her emotions under control. "But, Sadie, maybe it would be best if your father found someone else to stay with you when we get back to Mooresville. I…I can't be sure it won't happen again, not after today." She lifted her head and gave him that straight-forward, challenging gaze of hers he was coming to know so well. "I understand if you think it would be best to find Sadie a new…friend. One that can look after her without your worrying what might happen whenever you leave the house."

"No," Sadie said. She handed Puddles to Cassie and reached across to grab his hand in both of her smaller ones. "I don't want another friend, Dad. Not another nanny who's almost as old as Grandma. I want Cassie to stay with me. If…if she gets scared like this again, I'll know what to do. I'll watch over her, too. We'll watch over each other. Please, Dad. Don't let her quit. Please."

"It's up to Cassie," Ethan said, looking down at Sadie's hands, then up to her earnest, pleading face. He didn't want Cassie to leave them, either. Not this soon. But what if something like this happened again and he was away? Just as he'd been when Laura died. Too far away to help. Too far away to make a difference.

Cassie kept watching his face, must have read the in-decision in his eyes. She kept her face composed, but she stroked the little dog with still-trembling fingers. "This is the worst attack I've had in several months," she told them both. "The therapist warned me I'd have some setbacks along the way, but that the attacks would get further apart and last for a shorter time, and someday they would go away altogether. I…I just don't know when that will be."

"I want what's best for my daughter," Ethan said, choosing his words very carefully. Cassie was in far too fragile a condition at the moment to add to her stress by speaking with his heart, instead of his intellect. What he wanted to tell her was that he would take care of both of them, her and his daughter. That he wouldn't fail her, or Sadie, as he had failed Laura. That he wanted her to stay with them not only for the duration of Sadie's school break but…for the rest of their lives.

No, it was too soon to say such things. Too soon for her. Too soon for him.

Instead, he said, "Sadie is very mature for her age. She has already offered to watch over you while you watch over her. That sounds like a reasonable solution to me." He held her gaze, smiled, saw just the stirring of an answering smile touch the corners of her mouth. "Stay with us…both… for as long as you want to."

HE ANSWERED on the second ring. Cassie wondered if he had been sleeping with his phone in his hand. "Ethan, it's Cassie," she whispered into her cell phone. Sadie was curled up on the sofa bed in the salon of the motor home, Puddles lying on the pillow between them, snoring gently.

"Cassie, is everything okay? Are you all right?" He didn't sound as if he had been wakened from a deep sleep in the middle of the night. Perhaps he hadn't been asleep at all?

"Yes, everything's fine," she said. "I'm sorry to wake you, but I don't know when we might have any private time for me to say what I have to say."

"What's bothering you?" She squeezed her eyes shut, blotting out the ambient light from the sodium vapor lamps that kept the motor-home lot bathed in a pink glow from sundown to first light. His voice was a low, gentle growl in her ear, and it sent shivers through her body that had nothing to do with the residual anxiety of her panic attack.

"I think we should talk some more about my caring for Sadie, given what happened today." She reached down and rubbed her leg. She'd twisted it sometime during the mad dash from Trey's fans and it still ached. When she'd finished talking to Ethan she would take a pain pill and then maybe she could relax enough to sleep. That was another thing the therapist had urged. Don't try to tough out the pain. You don't have to do it all alone.

"I thought we had settled that," Ethan said. She wondered if he was lying down or sitting up against the pillows as she was. She wondered who else on the team was sharing his motor home. She hadn't had any reason to ask him about his sleeping arrangements. It was none of her business, after all. But the woman inside her who was not all business wanted to know. "I trust you to watch over Sadie despite the possibility you might have another panic attack. That's the end of it as far as I'm concerned."

"I'm not sure I trust myself," she confessed. "I should have told you that from the beginning."

He was silent for a long moment. "I know how you feel," he said at last, perhaps lulled by the darkness and the distance between them into telling her things he would not have told her in the daylight. "I've had my own form of post-traumatic stress to deal with these past years. Only, when you're not in the military, I guess it's just plain, old-fashioned grief. I wasn't there when my wife died, Cassie. She was alone. Alone with Sadie. My in-laws found her after they couldn't get her to answer the phone. Sadie was barely three. Thank God she was still in her bed and hadn't wakened to cry out for Laura in the night."

"I'm sorry," Cassie whispered, gazing down at Sadie's golden hair in the half light. "So sorry."

"Laura hadn't been feeling well, but she'd put off going to the doctor until I could get back from Vegas—that's where we were racing that week. It was my first race as crew chief of a NASCAR Nationwide car. She didn't want me to miss my chance and, God help me, I didn't want to miss it, either. She had a blood clot in her leg. Sometime during the night it broke loose and went directly to her heart. She died almost instantly. She couldn't have been saved. I guess the doctors thought it would make it easier for me to know that. It didn't."

Cassie curled her hand more tightly around the phone that bound them together with an invisible cord of shared sorrow and pain. "Nothing makes that kind of guilt easier to bear," she said, speaking from the very depth of her heart. Two Marines had not made it through the ambush. Two of her own.

"No," he agreed, "but you were wiser than I was. I tried to tough it out, to work through my pain and grief on my own. It took a long time to forgive myself. You sought help. That's why I trust you to know if you're really in over your head looking after Sadie, even if you are prey to occasional doubts."

Did she trust herself? She wanted to think she did. She wanted to think today was an aberration, a small relapse, hopefully the last of its kind. Across the distance he seemed to read her mind.

"Cassie, if you need time to talk to someone, a professional, we'll find it."

She looked inward, searched for that cold, hard stone of fear and anxiety that had weighed her down for so long, even before she left Iraq. It wasn't there, or only tiny fragments of it, anyway. "Thank you," she said. "But no. Not now. Not unless…" She stumbled to a halt. "Ethan—"

"No more buts, Cassie. What's the Marine Corps motto? *Semper Fidelis?*"

"Always faithful," Cassie murmured.

"That's what you are, Cassie, always faithful. Always there for the ones who trust you, for the ones who need you. Even after less than a week of knowing you, I'm convinced of that." She heard a thread of a smile seep into his voice. "Now go to sleep, Marine. We've got a big day ahead of us tomorrow."

CHAPTER TEN

IT WAS A SOUND Ethan was not used to hearing in his home. Laughter. Women's laughter. He moved toward the source, drawn by the happiness in their voices. His house had been taken over by Connors women, he knew that much. It was the Monday after the Phoenix race and traditionally a day off for most race teams. He had gone to the shop, anyway, to run some computer simulations and start working on his pit strategy for Talladega the coming week, but Sadie had stayed home with Cassie, Lelah, Puddles and Mia, who had joined them for the day.

He wondered what they were up to, giggling and talking among themselves. He didn't have long to find out. The quartet was grouped in his sterile, ice-palace-white living room, and they had been moving furniture. A lot of furniture. What had brought that on? He eavesdropped for a moment or two before making his presence known.

"This conversation grouping would look so much more inviting with an area rug to anchor it," Cassie was saying, the sweeping motion of her hands encompassing the wall of windows and the fieldstone fireplace that dominated the room. "These floors are beautifully finished, but they add to the chill of the room."

"This place definitely reminds me of an ice rink," Mia chimed in. She and Sadie were seated side by side on the portion of the gigantic white sectional that remained in front of the fireplace. Puddles was curled up in Sadie's lap, sleeping, as was his wont.

"And you can't watch the TV, either, because the light from the windows is always shining right on the screen. I asked Dad if we could take it up to my bedroom and he said no, that I didn't need a sixty-inch plasma screen TV in my bedroom."

"I agree with your father on that point," Lelah said. She was sitting in one of the two prissy little high-back chairs that were the room's only other furnishings, her elbows propped on her knees, her chin in her hands as she surveyed the unsuitable decor with a jaundiced eye. "This place is hopeless."

"Not hopeless," Cassie said. She had her back to him, her legs slightly spread, her arms crossed over her chest, surveying her objective. "But it needs work."

"It needs a miracle," Mia muttered under her breath to Sadie. His daughter giggled delightedly.

"I like what we've done with the furniture," Cassie went on, "but I don't think we should move the entertainment center without Ethan's permission. Most men are really finicky about their electronics."

"You're in luck. I'm not one of them," Ethan said not altogether truthfully as he advanced into the room.

Four heads and four sets of eyes swiveled in his direction. All three of the Connors women had hazel eyes, but only Cassie's were shot through with gold, like sunlight dancing on river water. "I bought the entertainment center," he continued, "because it's the only thing that holds its own against that Moby Dick of a couch."

"Dad, you're home early," Sadie said, waiting for Puddles to wake up and jump off her lap before she hopped up and came bouncing over to him, the little dog right on her heels. He wrapped his daughter in a bear hug, but kept a wary eye on Puddles. The Yorkie sniffed the tip of his shoe, gave a yip and sat down on his haunches, his tongue lolling out of his mouth in greeting.

"Will you look at that!" Mia said. "He…he's behaving. He's like a different dog." She had swiveled in her seat and put both feet on the floor, smiling a shy greeting. "Hello, Chief," she said.

"Hello, Ethan," Lelah warbled.

Cassie only nodded. "We'll put everything back the way it was," she said. "But Sadie was complaining about the glare on the TV screen…"

"I know. I heard that part. And I have no objection at all to moving the TV. I should have thought of it myself." He moved to the wall that the living room and dining room shared. "I take it this is where y'all think it should go?" The enterprising quartet had placed two sections of the white sofa in a V-shape in front of the blank wall. They'd placed the faux sheepskin rug that had lain in front of the fireplace between the sectionals, as well as one of the several glass-and-wrought-iron tables that littered the room. "Right about here, I suppose?" he said, spreading his hands.

"I think the three of us can manage to move it if you take the TV out first."

"It's pine. Not as heavy as oak or maple. We'll do okay." He didn't make the mistake of suggesting he call a couple of guys from the shop to help. If Cassie said she and Mia could handle their end of it, they could. The relocation went off without a hitch.

"We're good to go then," Cassie said as she surveyed their handiwork. She had been a little skittish around him since their middle-of-the-night phone call. He felt a little skittish himself, if he was honest. He hadn't spoken that intimately, that unguardedly, with a woman since Laura. It took some getting used to.

"Anything else you want moved while we're at it?"

Cassie forgot her shyness and locked her gaze with his. "Don't offer if you don't mean it," she said. Vintage Cassie. He worked hard not to smile.

"I never offer what I can't deliver."

"We'd like the Oriental rug from the dining room," she said without a moment's hesitation. "It has a beautiful pattern and colors, but it's almost completely hidden underneath that mammoth dining table of yours."

"It's not mine, remember, I told you that the first day. It came with the house. Our furniture is upstairs in the bedrooms and in the den."

"That gorgeous leather furniture in the den would look marvelous with the rug," Lelah said, rising from the spindly-legged chair carefully. "Such a rich, dark blood-red."

"My in-laws gave it to us when they sold their house and moved into their condo. I don't think anyone's sat in it since we moved here, right, doodlebug?"

"The TV's in here," she said as if that explained everything.

"Is there anything else I can contribute to this decorating project?" he asked.

"There's nothing else in the house we like," Sadie said with devastating candor. "We did a recon this morning. Mia thinks we need to take a road trip to the Frugal Decorator. Can I borrow your credit card?"

"Sadie." Mia looked stricken. "I…I didn't mean… Sorry, Chief," she finished miserably. Ethan waved off the apology.

"The Frugal Decorator? What's that?"

"A decorating warehouse in Charlotte," Cassie said, diverting his attention from her sister, or so she thought. She needn't have bothered, for he wasn't paying any attention to Mia at all. Every sensor in his body was focused on her. "But Sadie's getting ahead of herself. We have no intention of buying your furniture for you. We're only trying to make this room more comfortable."

He gave the room a skeptical glance. "You'd need a fairy godmother to do that without spending a bundle of money."

"Which we do not intend to do," Cassie repeated.

He tried a different tack. "Okay, how about a road trip to buy a few things to bring the temperature in this room to above freezing? You know, pillows or new lamps or something." He ran out of ideas at that point.

"Pillows would be a start," Lelah said, sounding hopeful.

"Your lamps are fine," Cassie said. "The best thing we've got going for us." He gave the table lamps a quick look. Twisted brass columns, granite bases and white shades. With fringe. He hated them. As if picking up on his thoughts, she added, "You won't recognize them with different shades. And a couple of throws would warm up the sectional."

"And some sheers for the windows," Mia chimed in. "The hardware's beautiful, but those white drapes are so bland. All they do is block the view."

"None of that sounds as if it will bankrupt me," Ethan said, reaching into his back pocket for his wallet.

"Road trip!" Sadie giggled and clapped her hands. She began to dance around in a circle, Puddles yapping at her heels. She skipped over and plucked the credit card from his hand. "This place will be so awesome when we're done. We've been talking about what to do with it all morning. I can't wait. I wish you'd come along."

He held up both hands as though warding off an attack. "No way. You guys are strictly on your own."

"WHAT DO YOU THINK, Dad?" Sadie asked her father six hours later as they sat side by side in front of the big-screen TV in Ethan's revamped living room. "I told you it would be awesome." She yawned hugely. "'Scuse me," she said, popping her hand over her mouth.

"I am impressed," Ethan said. "I am *very* impressed."

"And we didn't max out your credit card," Cassie said, looking around her. She was sitting on the other side of the cannibalized sectional, as tired as Sadie and more than a little stiff and sore from all the pushing and lifting, but feeling very satisfied with her efforts. The spindly-legged chairs had been banished to the alcove formed by the big bay window, draped in the same fabric—a translucent brown silk—that had replaced the generic white sheers. The chairs now flanked a gate-legged wooden table that had been languishing in the upstairs hallway. The table, polished and gleaming, held a slender glass vase filled with polished stones and dried grasses that Lelah had plucked off a closeout table for pennies.

"That's even more impressive," he said, grinning. "Seriously, Cassie, thank you very much. I never thought I'd be comfortable in this room, but now I've changed my mind."

His praise washed over her like sunshine, warming her inside and out.

"It still needs a lot of work." She took a moment to gaze around the big room again. There was nothing they could do about the stark white walls on such short notice, but she was hoping Ethan would opt for a strong, warm color for them when it came time to paint—cinnamon, maybe, or even a rich cocoa brown.

"We had a great time shopping," Sadie chattered on. "I saw all kinds of things I'd like to buy for my bedroom. I'd like to try a more contemporary look now that I'm almost a teenager." Ethan raised one brow, his eyes widening in surprise. Cassie looked down at her hands for a moment so she didn't insult Sadie by letting her see the smile she couldn't restrain.

"We'll check a few decorating magazines out of the library so you can get some ideas," she suggested. "How does that sound?"

"Great." Sadie yawned again and snuggled close to her father's side. "I'm really tired," she said. "But a good tired." Moments later she was fast asleep.

"Are these the same tables that have always been here?" Ethan asked, touching one of the wrought-iron legs with the toe of his shoe.

"The very ones."

"I'm glad you held the line on tablecloths," Ethan said. "I've never been fond of them."

"I thought you might not be," she said, inordinately pleased at her insight. Instead, she'd chosen thin bamboo mats from the warehouse's patio-living area to cover the glass tabletops and eliminate their icy reflections. She'd splurged on a couple of big wooden bowls filled with carved fruit and polished rocks to accessorize them, some matching wooden pedestals to hold pillar candles for the mantel, and a gigantic silk fern to fill the empty maw of the fireplace for the summer months. All in all she was pleased with the effect.

"How many pillows did you buy?" Ethan whispered, flicking his hand along the length of the transformed white couches.

Cassie laughed quietly. "About two dozen, I think. Sadie picked out most of them and she was having such a good time doing it, I didn't have the heart to rein her in. Most of them were in the two-for-one aisle. You have the makings of a real bargain hunter there."

"That's my girl," he said, shifting the sleeping child a little closer to his side.

Cassie had to swallow a sudden lump in her throat. He hadn't shown such easy affection for his daughter a week ago. Things were moving in the right direction for the two of them. "There was barely room for her in the back seat of my car on the way home we bought so many," she continued, hoping her voice didn't betray the emotion she was feeling. "She has a great eye for color."

All the colors of the rainbow were represented in Sadie's choices, or more precisely, the colors of the gorgeous Oriental rug Ethan had rolled up and carried in from the dining room: persimmon, gold, red, sapphire and emerald green. Coupled with the dark red leather couch and matching pair of wing chairs they'd shifted from the unused den, the rug made an inviting conversation area in front of the fireplace. Once he had time to find some decent artwork for the walls, the room would be more than okay. It would be perfect.

"You ought to do this for a living," he said.

She shook her head. "I'd like to be my own boss, but that takes capital and I don't have any. Nope. I'm looking for a job with two weeks' paid vacation and health benefits."

"This could be your job, Cassie. I could meet those terms if you'd stay on with us after Sadie's spring break is over."

She took her time answering. If she spoke too soon the words would tumble out of her mouth just as Sadie's did when she was excited. Stay. But for how long? Long enough to lose her heart to Ethan's daughter? To lose her heart to the man himself?

She stood up so quickly the room spun around her for a moment. "I'm not sure that would be a good idea, Ethan. I have my mother and sister's future to think about, as well as my own. As much as I care for Sadie, as much as I love being with her, she's going to grow up very soon. She won't need me then."

He didn't rise when she did. He couldn't without disturbing the sleeping child. He stayed where he was, calm, still, solid as the bedrock deep beneath the house. "Sit down, Cassie," he said, his voice no less commanding for its gentleness. "I won't pressure you. The decision is yours."

She did sit down, but gingerly, perching on the edge of the seat. "I would like to stay, Ethan," she said. "But I can't." There was too much danger of becoming too involved with both Ethan and his daughter, too much danger of having her heart break when she had to leave. No. She couldn't stay permanently, no matter how much she might long to.

He frowned a little but didn't press his point. "I have a favor to ask you."

"What?" She clasped her hands together wondering what was coming.

"Will you come to Talladega with Sadie for the race next weekend?"

"Talladega?"

"Yes. You wouldn't be staying in the infield, though. Adam and Trey have offered me the use of a motor home. There's already a spot reserved for it in the owners' and drivers' lot. I'll be staying with the team in a hotel, where we reserve a block of rooms every year," Ethan said.

"I'd be happy to watch over her right here," Cassie said. It was tempting, though, the idea of seeing another race so soon. The Saturday-night race at Phoenix had been an exhilarating experience for both Sadie and her. And Trey had finished third—his best showing since Speedweeks at Daytona. But Talladega was in a league by itself when it came to stock car racing.

"I want her with me, Cassie. I'm realizing more every day how close I came to losing contact with her. We were growing apart. Martha and Ford have been hinting at it for a while, but I didn't let myself believe it until the nanny broke her leg and I was forced to face the truth."

"She loves you with all her heart, Ethan. That will never change."

"I want to make sure she knows I love her just as much. I don't want to waste any of the days we have together. Please say you'll come."

How could she turn down a plea she recognized as coming from his very core? "Yes, I'll come," she said.

"Thank you, Cassie," he said, rising, Sadie cradled in his arms. "And thank you for what you did today." He looked around the softly lighted room once more. "You've helped us make this house closer to really being home."

CHAPTER ELEVEN

IT WAS HOT for April, but this was Alabama, not North Carolina, Cassie reminded herself. *Talladega.* Legendary NASCAR track. One of the superspeedways, where cars could reach speeds of more than 180 miles an hour. Their powerful engines could produce such momentum on the long straightaways that NASCAR had decreed that race-tracks like Daytona and Talladega required restrictor plates to slow the cars down to manageable speeds.

Manageable being a relative term in stock car racing, Cassie decided, as she and Sadie waited in their motor home for their escort.

The only problem was that they were waiting for Trey Sanford and not Ethan. Ethan was still in the garage area overseeing the final car checks before the NASCAR Sprint Cup Series race the next day. Trey, on the other hand, was basking in the glow of his NASCAR Nationwide Series win earlier in the afternoon.

He'd pulled some strings to get them passes. He would be escorting them to the Sanford Racing hauler and from there to one of the luxury boxes above the grandstands for a gathering of Greenstone Garden Centers employees who had won sales contests and were attending the race weekend at his sponsor's expense. Ethan and Trey were old hands in these kinds of social situations, but Cassie was not and she was nervous, but only butterflies-in-the-stomach kind of nervous, nothing serious.

There had been no lasting effects from her anxiety attack a week ago, and she was beginning to believe that her therapist had been right. She might have a setback now and then, but the worst was behind her. She prayed that was true.

It had been a good week for all of them. Ethan had made a point to be home early each evening to spend time with Sadie, and the girl was blossoming from the attention. On Wednesday they had been able to reach her grandparents on their cruise ship as they sailed up the Amazon. They had told her remarkable stories of pink dolphins swimming alongside the ship a thousand miles upriver from the ocean, and of going into the jungle where monkeys played in the trees while parrots as colorful as rainbows flew overhead, and of seeing a flock of butterflies as big as saucers and all the same brilliant blue as Sadie's eyes. Sadie had been so excited she and Ethan had stayed up together until almost midnight surfing the Internet for images to match Ford and Martha's descriptions.

Cassie's only disappointment was that Lelah had come down with a spring cold and hadn't felt up to making the trip to Alabama. Puddles had stayed behind to keep her company, and Mia was in charge of looking after both of them.

"Trey's late," Sadie said. She was tapping away at her game screen with a stylus, taking care of her Zanies family, which she still did conscientiously, but with much less fervor as her days became filled with more adventurous activities. Cassie felt she could add that to her list of accomplishments, a small one compared to seeing the progress Ethan had made with his daughter, but satisfying nonetheless.

"He's only a few minutes late."

"Will there be kids at this party?" Sadie was always on the lookout for new friends. She was coming out of her shell so quickly that sometimes even Cassie was caught off guard by how much of a social butterfly the girl had become. Cassie, too, was becoming a lot more social. Yesterday morning she and Sadie had had coffee with Sophia Murphy and Patsy Grosso. When she left the Grosso motor home her knowledge of NASCAR's private side had expanded by leaps and bounds, and she was afraid her waistline had, too, tempted as she'd been by the homemade muffins and pastries Patsy had plied them with.

"Possibly—I don't know for sure. It's for employees and their families, so maybe there will be."

"I hope so. It's kind of boring without Dana and Jamie here, but they're coming to Richmond next week."

"That's nice. When did you talk to them?"

"E-mail," she said, not looking up from the screen. "This motor home is awesome. It's got everything."

Including a whirlpool bathtub surrounded by mirrored walls. Pure decadence. Cassie had used it both nights they'd stayed in the motor home. She wished she could take it with her when they left.

A knock sounded on the door. Cassie opened it to allow Trey inside. "Ready to rumble, ladies?" he asked, smiling that megawatt smile of his. His eyes swept over both of them, returning to give Cassie a second scrutiny. He gave a long, low whistle. "Very nice."

"Thank you, kind sir." She had chosen her dress with

care. It was one she seldom wore, the product of a shopping spree soon after she'd returned from Iraq when she'd wanted and needed to feel pretty and feminine again. The bodice was fitted with a square neckline and cap sleeves. The skirt was short, not short enough to reveal her scars, but far enough above her knees to qualify as sexy, according to her sister. She'd piled her hair on top of her head and secured it with her favorite tortoiseshell combs.

Only her shoes spoiled the effect—at least temporarily. She was wearing a pair of walking shoes that had seen better days, but she had a pair of strappy little sandals in her tote that she intended to change into when the first opportunity presented itself.

"Ready," Sadie said, jumping up off the couch. She tucked her game into her tote and grabbed her Sanford Racing cap and matching shades.

Cassie thought about trying to talk her into the cute straw hat they'd bought from a souvenir vendor the night before but decided against it. Let her wear what she wanted. She probably wasn't the only girl running around in a ruffled sundress and a baseball cap.

"Have you been enjoying yourself?" Trey asked politely as they piled into a golf cart and glided off toward the grandstand area.

"We've been having fun," Sadie said. "But I miss Puddles. I'm going to ask my dad for a dog when we get back home. I'm old enough to take care of a puppy. Especially if Cassie helps me house-train him." Cassie's heart squeezed painfully when she realized that sooner or later she would have to tell Sadie she wouldn't be there to help her with dog training even if Ethan agreed to her request.

It shouldn't hurt so much to walk away, she told herself. *I've only been caring for her less than two weeks. Not long enough to fall in love with her,* but the ache in her heart refused to go away.

Trey halted the golf cart in a small corral-type area at the beginning of the row of titanic haulers. The big rigs were parked in laser-straight rows just as they had been the week before in Phoenix. The scene before them wasn't so very different from the desert racetrack, but the weather certainly was. It was hot and humid and the threat of thunderstorms hung heavy in the air, as did the smell of smoke from hundreds of campfires in the infield and surrounding campgrounds. "We'll walk from here," Trey said. "No room to park the cart closer to the hauler. Glad to see you're wearing sensible shoes."

"You noticed, huh?" Cassie said, feeling comfortable enough in his company to tease just a little. He had been the perfect gentlemen all weekend and didn't seem inclined to renew his flirtatious behavior of the week before.

"Is that where we're meeting my dad?" Sadie asked, shouldering her tote just as Cassie did.

"Yep," said Trey, already moving briskly. All the drivers walked fast, she noticed. If they didn't they got mobbed, just the way Trey had last week. She looked around her, observing heads turning in their direction. She reached for Sadie's hand, but only as a precaution. She wasn't afraid. She wasn't even nervous, she realized, just on the alert.

A couple of reporters wearing headphones like those the pit crews wore to communicate with each other, carrying microphones and trailing cameramen with big video cameras on their shoulders, caught sight of Trey and headed in their direction.

"Hell," Trey muttered. "Here we go and me without my publicist to keep me from putting my foot in my damned mouth."

"Trey, how's it going, buddy? Got a minute for a couple of questions?" the reporter who reached them first asked.

"Sure," Trey said, sounding as if he had nothing better to do in the world than give sound bites to track reporters, even though he'd just finished an hour-long news conference not long before.

"Great driving in the NASCAR Nationwide race today."

"Great car. It's too bad Shelley came down with that stomach bug, but I was glad for the chance to get back in a NASCAR Nationwide car. Winning the race was the icing on the cake. I've got to thank everyone at Sanford Racing and all our NASCAR Nationwide sponsors for giving me the time of my life today."

"You qualified fifth for tomorrow's NASCAR Sprint Cup race. That's your best starting position this season. Do you feel like you've got the wind at your back now? Are you confident the slump is over?"

"Something's changed, that's for sure. I don't discount good luck, but I'm more inclined to give credit to my teammates here at the track and back at the shop. Ethan Hunt's one hell of a crew chief and he's been workin' his butt off to get this car where it is today. I'm just going to drive the wheels off it tomorrow and we'll see what happens then." He grinned into the camera. "I sure wouldn't mind making this a twofer this weekend."

Another three or four reporters had hurried up, microphones thrust out to catch Trey's every word. Cassie could sense he'd begun to relax as the questions remained focused on his driving and not on his private life. Cassie didn't relax, though. She remained alert, old skills coming to the fore, as she held Sadie's hand lightly in hers.

"Hey, Trey," one of the newcomers, a woman, called out as she wriggled her way to the front of the pack. She was wearing a knock-off driver's uniform with a cable-sports-channel logo embroidered over her chest. "Got a minute?"

"Nope," Trey said with a wolfish grin. "Gotta get moving. I'm delivering these lovely ladies to my crew chief, and all of you know what a stickler he is for being on time."

"Still smarting from the fine he levied on you for being late for last week's team meeting?" the reporter purred, moving forward aggressively, the others crowding close to hear the give-and-take. "You were late, weren't you? Got docked by your crew chief, right? Was it because your flight from Mexico was delayed? Or was it the delay caused by the woman you went there to see?"

Sadie stumbled as one of the cameramen swung around to register Trey's reaction to the provocative questions and bumped into her. "Look out, kid," he growled, barely glancing her way. Cassie didn't hesitate. She wasn't wearing combat boots, but her running shoes were heavy-soled and sturdy. Without a moment's hesitation she brought her heel down on his instep with all the force she could muster. The man yelped and jumped backward, elbowing the reporter standing beside him, his microphone thrust forward to capture Trey's response. The collision started a chain reaction in which recorders and micro-phones went flying.

"Good one," Trey mouthed in her direction. "You okay?" he asked, turning serious in a heartbeat, his eyes boring into hers.

"I'm fine," Cassie said, and she meant it. She wasn't panicked. She wasn't scared, but she was really, really mad.

"Good. Take Sadie. Go now."

Cassie tightened her grip on Sadie's hand. The girl was trembling, but her expression wasn't fearful, only concerned. "I'll take care of you, Cassie," she said, squeezing her hand hard. "I promised I would."

"We'll take care of each other." With those words, as quickly as she'd spoken them, she crossed the line from caring about Sadie to loving her as if she were her own. Cassie began to urge her charge out of range of the reporters, but they were already beginning to regroup, and one or two had taken notice of them moving away.

A tanned, fit man about her own age, with a smile that revealed a set of perfect white teeth, got between them and Trey. He wasn't wearing any kind of uniform, but a casual shirt and sharply pressed khakis. He didn't have a cameraman in tow, either, but he was sporting what looked like an expensive digital camera on a strap around his neck. His credentials were clipped to his shirt pocket and he carried a digital recorder in his hand. "Hello, who have we here?" He gave Sadie a quick glance, then returned his gaze to Cassie. "Ethan Hunt's daughter, right? But who are you?"

"No comment," Cassie said, the words clipped.

"That was pretty quick thinking on your part. Ashley Bainer's cameraman is going to be limping all weekend after the move you put on him. I'd stay out of his viewfinder for a few days if I were you."

"Thanks for the advice. I'll do that. Now step aside or you'll end up the same way," Cassie said.

"C'mon. Just a couple of quotes for tomorrow's *Racing Insider*'s Internet edition. Are you the woman Trey's been flying off to Mexico to see?"

"I said let us pass," she hissed, and saw the man's eyes widen as she balled her free hand into a fist and waved it under his nose. "Now!"

"Hey, okay." He raised his hand as if to ward off an attack, laughing as he did so, seemingly unable to believe a woman as small as Cassie could really do him any harm. "Sure. No problem," he said, grinning indulgently.

His condescension angered her even more. She ground her teeth and narrowed her eyes, ready to give him a piece of her mind even though Ethan's warning not to talk to the press echoed in her mind with ringing clarity.

"You heard the lady. No interviews with my daughter or her friend." The blogger or reporter—or whatever he was—whirled around to find himself staring at a very angry crew chief. Ethan was wearing his team uniform and a dark blue ball cap that shadowed his eyes but did nothing to mask the hard line of his jaw and the angry set of his mouth.

"Daddy!" Sadie called out.

Reinforcements. The cavalry had arrived. "He's having trouble understanding the meaning of 'no comment,'" Cassie said, glaring at the reporter.

Ethan glanced past them to Trey, still surrounded by the media scrum but leading them away at a trot toward Justin Murphy's Turn-Rite Tools hauler, where Sophia's new husband, who had obviously been watching what was happening, deflected their attention long enough for Trey to slip inside and disappear. Justin raised his hand in a half salute and followed Trey into the privacy of the hauler. Justin and Trey might be rivals on the track, but when it came to bailing fellow drivers out of a tight spot, these guys formed their own band of brothers, Cassie noted with approval.

Ethan swung Sadie up into his arms. "Okay, doodlebug?"

"I'm fine. Cassie, are you okay?"

"Good to go," she said, touching Sadie's cheek.

Ethan gave her a long, assessing gaze, then nodded. *"Semper Fi,"* he said so quietly only she could hear.

"Semper Fi." Cassie fell into step beside him, but their tormentor refused to give up, keeping pace, walking backward as he talked.

"Chief Hunt, despite how well he finished last week and the way he drove in the NASCAR Nationwide race today, how distracting have Trey Sanford's late-night trips to Mexico been to the team?"

"No comment," Ethan barked. A half-dozen more strides and they would be at the hauler. Cassie kept walking, kept her mouth shut, although she itched to give the pushy man a piece of her mind.

"Hey, lady, give me a break. Are you the reason Trey's sticking so close to home all of a sudden? I caught a glimpse of you at Phoenix last week. Then you popped up in Victory Lane this afternoon, and Trey looked mighty glad to see you." He spread his hands. "Now, here you are again. Three's a charm." There was a leer in his voice if not on his face. He lifted his camera as though to snap a shot of Cassie.

Ethan stopped dead in his tracks. Sadie dropped her

head onto his shoulder and buried her face in his neck. Cassie took a step forward, but Ethan's free hand flicked out and circled her wrist, holding her still, holding her close. So close she could feel the heat of his thigh burn through the thin fabric of her dress. He leaned slightly forward and bared his teeth in what might have been a smile—on a wolf, a very angry wolf.

The reporter dropped his camera as if it had suddenly burned his hand. "She's not a lady," Ethan said, "she's a U.S. Marine, and I suggest you apologize to her right here and right now, before she decides to pound your miserable carcass into the dirt. Understand?"

She took a step forward as if she had every intention of doing exactly as Ethan said.

The reporter stammered a little in his haste to make amends. "Sure. No harm intended. Just doing my job. People want to know why Trey's down in the points standing. Maybe he's not ready for the Show? Maybe he should be back in the NASCAR Nationwide car full-time? Or maybe he needs a new crew chief?" he said, getting a little of his own back.

"If you think that's the case, you'd better talk to Adam Sanford. He does the hiring and firing around here." Ethan turned his back and marched into the interior of the hauler, Cassie following behind, Sadie still in his arms.

"He can't come in here with us, can he, Daddy?" she whispered.

"Not unless he wants his credentials yanked and his butt in jail," Ethan said. Opening the door at the end of the narrow hallway, he deposited Sadie on the padded bench that was built into a corner of the crowded space at the very front of the trailer. "Are you okay, doodlebug?" he asked, brushing her fine, blond hair away from her cheek, tucking the strands behind her ear.

"Yes," she said. "But for a minute I was afraid I'd get squashed when that guy almost knocked me down. But mostly I was afraid for Cassie. You're really all right, aren't you?" she asked anxiously.

"I'm really, really okay, Sadie," Cassie said, sliding onto the bench seat beside Sadie and giving the girl a hug.

"I'm glad of that," she said, hugging back.

"I think Sadie would appreciate a drink of something cool," Cassie said, blinking hard to hold back a quick sting of tears.

"Sure," Ethan said, and opened a small refrigerator tucked under a counter on which sat a couple of laptops, a TV monitor like the ones in the pits and a bank of telephones. "Here you go. One for each of you," he said, twisting off the caps.

"Thanks." Their hands brushed momentarily as she took the water bottle, and the contact reminded her of the strength of his hard-muscled body so near her own when they'd faced down the reporter. The heat and clarity of the memory made her blush. She hoped he didn't notice.

Sadie gulped down some water and then yelped, "Ouch. Brain freeze." She rubbed her forehead, her face screwed up in a grimace of pain.

"Slow down, doodlebug," Ethan cautioned. "You'll make yourself sick to your stomach and then we won't be able to go to the party."

Sadie turned to Cassie. "Would you really have stomped that guy into the dirt?" she asked, setting her half-empty bottle of water on the table in front of her. "Do they teach you to do that in the Marines?"

"They do," Cassie assured her.

"Awesome." Sadie's stomach chose that moment to rumble. "I'm hungry," she said. "Will they have anything good to eat at the party?"

"Let me check with Pete and see if it's safe to go back outside," Ethan said. The storm clouds darkening his face had cleared away, receding to the depths of his blue eyes. "Be back in a minute." He disappeared through the door.

"This place is cool," Sadie said, looking around with bright, curious eyes. "I've never been in the hauler before."

"I've never been anywhere like this before, either," Cassie said, satisfying her own curiosity about the mobile nerve center of Sanford Racing. Ethan had left his hat behind. It was sitting atop a pile of computer printouts on the counter near one of the flat screen monitors. She had the silliest adolescent desire to pick it up and hold it to her heart.

How ridiculous was that? She was almost twenty-nine years old. She'd never behaved that way even when she was head over heels in puppy love with Trenton Carlisle, the captain of the freshman football team.

"I'm still hungry," Sadie said. "If they're only going to have little sandwiches and pieces of cheese on toothpicks at this party, I'd rather go back to the motor home and get something good to eat."

Cassie was beginning to feel a little tired as the adrenaline jolt of her confrontation with the media began to dissipate. She wasn't in the mood for a party, either. She smiled and held out her hand. "Sounds like a plan. Let's find your dad and see if he'll take us home."

CHAPTER TWELVE

"Is SHE ASLEEP?" Cassie asked as Ethan came out of the small sleeping area of the motor home, where Sadie was tucked up in the bottom of a set of bunk beds.

"Out like a light," he said quietly, pulling shut the pocket door that closed the area off from the kitchen and salon.

"It's been another big day for her," she said, smiling at him from where she was curled up on the couch in the section of the living area that pulled out to form a kind of alcove. She was wearing flannel pants and a thin cotton hoodie in a kind of berry pink that matched the sunburn on her nose. He almost pointed that out, but changed his mind at the last moment. Women were funny about things like that.

"A big day for you, too." He sat down on a chair next to the couch and stretched his legs out in front of him. On the opposite side of the unit another pop-out made extra room for a dining table and six chairs. He liked this motor home. It was roomy and comfortable. He'd never owned a motor home of his own. Usually he stayed with the team in a hotel as close to the track as possible. But now that he had Sadie with him, maybe he ought to start looking for a rig of his own.

"Is that your tactful way of asking if I've had any

delayed effects from the dustup with that jerk earlier?" Cassie asked, cradling a mug of coffee laced with an ounce of mellow Irish whiskey. The whiskey had been his idea, but she hadn't objected.

"It might be," he said carefully. He picked up his own glass, whiskey neat, and took a sip. He'd told her he'd left the sponsor's party to come back to tuck Sadie in, and he had. But he'd also wanted to check on Cassie.

She held out her hand. "Steady as a rock." She smiled and it lit up the room. "I'm fine, really I am."

"I'm sorry you missed the party," he said when he could breathe again.

"I'm not, unless they had those really big shrimp. Did they? I love shrimp."

"Mammoth," he said, spreading his thumb and finger three inches apart. "Not to mention the kind of stuff you women like. Lots of green and leafy little sandwiches and crackers with bits and pieces of twigs and branches on top of the cream cheese. Green cream cheese," he said, making a face. Trey's sponsor, Greenstone Garden Centers, was big into organic foods so the menu choices weren't all that un- expected—or that bad. "You would probably have liked the chocolate fountain, though. Never thought I'd live to see a chocolate fountain at a NASCAR race."

"Guess times are changing," Cassie said with a grin. "Sadie and I had a good time right here."

"Even if you ended up eating hot dogs roasted over a gas burner, instead of jumbo shrimp and a chocolate fountain?"

"We had an indoor picnic. With s'mores for dessert," Cassie said, taking another sip of her coffee. "So I got my chocolate fix. Besides, in case you haven't noticed, I'm the kind of woman who doesn't mind eating hot dogs charred over a gas burner and washing it down with a cherry soda."

"I've noticed," he said, watching her expressive face above the rim of his glass. He noticed everything about Cassie now, but mostly he noticed how he wanted to take her in his arms and kiss her.

"She'd never done that before," Cassie continued, either not hearing what he'd said—or pretending not to. "I can't count the times Mom and Mia and I had indoor picnics when the two of us were kids."

Ethan detected a more serious note beneath her words and suspected Lelah's indoor picnics were a way of disguising the fact that she couldn't afford more expensive entertainment or restaurant meals for her children.

"Indoor picnics aren't something that my in-laws do in the normal course of events," he said, taking his cue to keep some distance—at least for the moment. "Ford and Martha are loving grandparents who would do anything for Sadie, but their idea of a casual evening is a restaurant without white linen tablecloths and a maître d'."

"Do you think they'll regret not having Sadie with them as much after they return from their cruise? They must be very attached to her."

"They want what's best for Sadie and they know they're not up to raising a teenager. Sadie will be able to visit them as often as she wants. She just won't be staying there for days at a time."

"What about Sadie attending the boarding school they've chosen for her? She wants very badly to go to regular school like the Paulson girls."

Ethan frowned. He had no objection to the Wentworth

School, per se. Sadie was receiving an excellent education there, but this was her last year, and though in the past, even as short a time as two weeks ago, he might have let Ford and Martha influence his opinion on boarding school, that was no longer the case. "I'll speak to them about it. I want to give them a chance to get used to the idea that she won't be attending Laura's old school. They're good people. They'll come around to my way of thinking when they see how eager Sadie is to transfer to public school."

"Does that mean you're ready to be a full-time, always-there-for-her father?" Cassie tilted her head and studied him with that firm, unwavering gaze.

"I am. I've always meant to be the best father I could be. I just lost sight of the big picture for a while. It won't happen again."

"I believe you," she said after a moment. "But no matter how sincere you might be, it doesn't alter the fact that you are a NASCAR team crew chief. Your job is one of the most demanding I've ever seen. You can't do this parenting thing without help."

"I've already admitted I need help, Cassie." He set his glass on the table and leaned forward. His hands were clasped between his knees because he wanted so badly to reach out to her, but didn't dare for fear she'd shy away. "I'm saying it again. I need you to stay with us. Permanently."

"And if I have a message on my answering machine when we get back to Mooresville that my dream job just opened up and they want me there first thing Monday morning, what will you do then?"

"I won't shanghai your sister into taking over your job," he said, letting a smile find its way to the corners of his mouth.

She smiled, too. "I'm not so sure of that."

"I'd match any offer this hypothetical employer made you. And I can promise you I'd never run off to Nepal to find myself." She gave a little gurgle of laughter as he took the lighthearted teasing one step further. "What would it take for you to change your mind and stay with my daughter…stay with us?" He wasn't teasing any longer. He'd never been more serious in his life.

She gave him another of those direct, assessing looks, the ones that peeled back the protective layers most people hid behind and looked into your mind and your heart and your soul to read your character and your intentions. "You don't have to offer me anything more than you already have."

"You mean you've changed your mind?"

"Sadie changed it for me," she said quietly, looking past him to the closed doorway behind which his child slept. "She has a very powerful hold on my heart."

He leaned forward and took the mug from her grasp, placing it on the narrow end table beside his chair. He took her hand in his, marveling at the strength he felt beneath the soft skin. "You'll stay?"

"As long as you need me."

He rubbed his thumb lightly over the delicate tracery of blue veins beneath the skin of her inner wrist. She shivered and curled her hand into a fist within the grip of his fingers. His breath caught and blood pounded in his ears. How long did he want her to stay? Until Sadie was in high school? College? *Forever?* "I want to do this right," he said, not sure if he was speaking aloud or only to himself, "but I don't want to do it alone."

She stiffened slightly. "What did you say?" she asked.

He met her gaze. Her eyes swirled with green and gold highlights in the low light from the single lamp burning at the far end of the sofa. "I don't want to be alone," he said again, his heart pounding hard in his chest. "I've been alone for more years than I care to remember."

"What are you asking me?" She spoke so softly he had to lean closer to hear her and that brought him close enough to be aware of her scent. Lemony this time, and beneath the scent of soap and shampoo, the warm sweetness of her skin, sun-kissed and womanly. He wanted her as a man wants a woman but it had been too long since he said such words aloud. They stuck in his throat, almost choking him.

"I don't know," he said finally, honestly. His head was spinning and his chest hurt. He knew now what it felt like for his driver to spin out of control at 180 miles an hour and end up against the inside wall. What did he want of her? For them to be together. A couple. A family? So in the end he simply spoke the truth, confused though his thoughts were. "I do know I want to keep you with us, Sadie and me."

"I told you I would stay. I won't leave, even if there is a job waiting for me when we get back home."

"Not that way." He took a leap of faith. "Marry me." He wasn't sure where exactly the words came from, or the courage to speak them. "Marry me and make us a family."

Her eyes grew big, rounded with surprise. Her hand jerked in his and then she tugged it free. He wanted to tighten his grip, to hold on to her, but he knew her well enough to know that would only make her more determined to be released.

"What did you say?" she asked.

He took a deep breath. "I just asked you to marry me," he said. Then he leaned closer and covered her mouth with his.

THE KISS WAS soul-shattering. Cassie's mind reeled with the unexpectedness of her reaction to his mouth on hers. Her ears were still ringing with the words he'd spoken, her heart thudded in her ears, and long tendrils of desire threaded through her veins into the very center of her being.

All those sensations flooding through her, and the only part of their bodies that were touching were their lips. What would it be like if he took her in his arms? He must have been thinking the same thing because he wrapped his arms around her and pulled her onto his lap, never breaking the contact of their mouths.

The kiss went on and on, as they learned each other, explored each other. Cassie let herself experience the contrast of male and female as she rested against the hard wall of his chest, felt the muscles through his uniform. She snuggled closer, let herself feel small and soft and utterly feminine, all woman, sensations she had locked away during her time in a combat zone and had continued to deny since coming home.

But no longer. Once released they refused to be caged again. She wound her arms around Ethan's neck and kissed him back, again and again, until they were both spent and out of breath.

"So you really asked me to marry you," she murmured as small strands of rational thought began to make their way to the forefront of her brain. She had started to dream of something like that, brief snatches of daydream, longer, more sensual night dreams of the two of them together, but she had never let herself believe it might really happen.

"I really did," he said, straightening up in the chair, still holding her close against him.

But dreams were not enough. Half-formed wishes were not enough. "Do you love me?" she asked. The warm glow of desire was fading away, and sanity had returned, leaving her chilled, and filled with sadness.

"I'm not sure I know what love is anymore, Cassie," he said, his hand gently stroking her hair. "I know that I've come to think of you as a friend. To value your honesty and your strength of character, to be grateful for the care and attention you show my daughter."

"In other words, you're offering me a new deal," she said, swallowing around the painful lump growing in her throat. She didn't want to be valued for her good qualities, not now, not when they were in each other's arms. She wanted to be loved. She wanted him to tell her he loved her with all his body and heart and soul, so that she could do the same.

"Cassie, I don't know what the hell I'm offering you. My name, my friendship. A better life for you and your mother. There's something between us. That kiss sure as hell proved that, but is it love? I don't know. I just don't know."

She raised her head. His face was a study in confusion and misery just like her heart. "Friendship? Security? No more? Then the answer is no," she whispered. "I want it all when I marry, Ethan. Fireworks and champagne bubbles and starry-eyed romance."

And she wanted all those things with him.

"I won't settle for anything else," she added.

"Then forgive me," he said, tracing the rough edge of his thumb over her cheek, wiping away the single tear that had escaped. "I can't offer you that just yet. Do me a favor and pretend I never opened my damned mouth."

"I can do that," she said, but she was lying to herself and to him.

CHAPTER THIRTEEN

"The results are official. Trey Sanford driving the No. 483 Greenstone Garden Centers car is the winner at Talladega! Second is Justin Murphy, followed by Kent Grosso…" That was all Ethan needed to hear. He pulled his headphones off and soaked in the cacophony of cheering, yelling team members and squealing tires as Trey turned doughnuts on the front straightaway.

Next stop: Victory Lane.

Adam Sanford slapped him on the shoulder and reached for his hand. "You did it, Ethan. Got my baby brother to Victory Lane in the Show. His first NASCAR Sprint Cup win. And at 'Dega, too—Trey's never been at his best in restrictor-plate races."

"Everything broke our way today." And it had. Trey had picked up a drafting partner early on in the race. He and Justin Murphy had started in the same row and managed to avoid both of the multicar pileups.

"I'm not saying luck didn't have something to do with it, but you called a hell of a race up here, you know that."

Ethan grinned, a mixture of triumph and relief. "You know he's liable to run out of gas on his victory lap, don't you?"

"It was that close?" Adam paused before climbing down from the box.

Ethan nodded. "If Justin hadn't stayed with him drafting to the end, we'd have been two laps short on fuel."

"I'll be damned." Adam clasped his hand. "Think you can pull off another race like this at Richmond next week?"

"I'm damned well going to try." Ethan wasn't as confident as he sounded. The team had come together this week, but he didn't know if the cohesiveness would carry over. All it would take was one bad pit stop or another series of engine problems like they'd suffered through earlier in the season, and they'd be back to square one. And then there was Trey. He'd toed the line these last two races, but Ethan was never certain what tomorrow would bring where his driver was concerned.

"Want me to send Pete up to the suite to escort Sadie and Ms. Connors to Victory Lane?" Adam asked as they descended into the midst of the milling, high-fiving team members and the already converging media.

"Uh, yeah, sure," he said when his boss gave him a surprised glance. "She got a real kick out of it yesterday."

"She'll get a bigger kick out of it today with you in the center of the hoopla."

He wasn't exactly certain when Sadie and Cassie arrived at the enclosed area of Victory Lane. He just looked up one moment and there they were. There *she* was. Cassie, pretty as a picture in a pale peach shirt and khaki slacks, her hair pushed up beneath a team cap, her skin glowing and her face wreathed in smiles.

Until she caught sight of him watching her and her smile faded away.

They were right in the middle of the hat dance, the obligatory round of team photos, each one taken with the team members wearing the hat of a different one of Trey's twenty-some sponsors. Ethan couldn't move away from where he was standing, couldn't wipe the fixed smile he'd been wearing for the past half hour off his face. He was stuck grinning like a fool when what he really wanted to do was beat his head against the side of Trey's car in frustration.

One of the PR people began passing out yet another set of hats and he grabbed his and jammed it on his head. He was hot and sweaty and reeked of the sickly sweet smell of champagne drying on his uniform. Even if he could get Cassie alone for a moment, he wasn't exactly in Prince Charming mode. And what would he tell her if he had the chance to be private? That he'd made a huge mistake the night before? That was a given.

What he couldn't tell her was that he was in love with her. She'd never believe him. How did you explain that you'd never believed in love at first sight? Never experienced it? Didn't know what the hell had hit you when it happened until it was too late? That one damned kiss had been the catalyst that had changed his world in a handful of minutes, but he hadn't the brains to figure it out himself—until later. When it was too late. Could anything sound more hokey?

She'd give him that long, straight stare, shake her head in pity and disgust and walk away.

More than likely forever.

THERE WERE thunderstorms out over the Gulf of Mexico. Cassie could see lightning flashes in the towering formations out the window of the plane. The sun was setting behind them as Adam Sanford's private jet headed back to Concord. Adam and his fiancée, Tara Dalton, another tall, leggy blonde, had invited Sadie and Cassie to fly home with them, rather than wait for the larger corporate jet Adam chartered for the team. Ethan had approved the plan so quickly she was certain he was as relieved as she was not to be cooped up together in an airplane for two hours.

She and Sadie had watched the race from one of the hospitality suites high above the racetrack where Adam himself escorted them before returning to the No. 483 car's pit. From that vantage point the pageantry and the spectacle had been overwhelming. The pride of country and family was evident in every aspect of the pre-race activities from the driver introductions to the invocation, the national anthem and the military flyover.

"Someday," Sadie had said, pointing to the hundreds of motor homes and campers that crowded the huge infield, "I'm going to have my own motor home and I'm going to come to the races and have flags flying from a pole and eat barbecue every meal for four whole days."

"I like that idea." Cassie had laughed, holding up her hand for a high five. "Don't forget to invite me to come along."

Sadie's eyes were shining with happiness and excitement as she'd slipped her arm around Cassie's waist and laid her head against her. "You can come with me to every single race."

Just that moment, the command "Start your engines" was given by a group of National Guard members, and Cassie's reply had been lost in the noise of forty-three powerful engines gunning to life.

As the race progressed Cassie had listened intently to the communications between Ethan and his driver over the room's sound system, tried to follow the bits and pieces of strategy they disclosed over the airwaves that could be and were monitored by countless fans, the media and opposing teams. She listened and absorbed and tried to make sense of it all, storing up questions for Mia when she returned home. Yet through it all Ethan's voice had sounded the same—always composed, always confident no matter the situation or the state of Trey's high-strung driver's nerves.

Even when the pileups happened, a spinning, rotating mass of a dozen out-of-control race cars shedding sheet metal and engine fluids as they careered across the track to skid to a stop along safety barriers and retaining fences, he'd never raised his voice.

He'd waited until Trey's spotter, high atop the grandstand, had guided Trey through the pall of smoke and steam from the wrecked cars and brought him safely to the other side before he started talking again—checking on Trey's well-being, asking his driver for an assessment of the car's condition, listening to Trey's feedback, electing to change all four tires, but only a top-off on the fuel tank to get him back out ahead of the leaders as the cars pitted under the yellow flag.

Ethan's strategy had paid off. Trey had drafted his way to the front with Justin Murphy, and then in the last two laps of the race, he'd slingshotted around his partner and taken the checkered flag. Cassie's throat had hurt from cheering, and Sadie had been beside herself with glee. She'd thrown herself into Cassie's arms and hugged her so tightly she'd winced. "We won! We won!" Sadie had cried.

"My dad and Trey won the race. I want to go congratulate them. I want to go to Victory Lane."

Pete Swenson had appeared just as she spoke to grant Sadie's wish. It had taken them quite a while to make their way to the restricted area around Victory Lane, but the hat dance was still going on, and Sadie, the team's new darling, had been swept up in the chaos—and into her handsome father's arms—while Cassie watched from the edges of the crowd.

That was when it had hit her that she had relegated herself to the edges of Ethan Hunt's life ever since she had refused his out-of-the-blue proposal of marriage the night before. She would remain Sadie's nanny and nothing more, because she was just too much of a coward to take the risk that what he had offered could someday blossom into a real marriage, a real love.

Cassie dropped her head against the window of the plane. What a mess it all was. Ethan had been too busy to spend time with them today. But tomorrow, tomorrow they would be thrown back into each other's company and she would have to keep her damned promise to herself, and to him, that she'd forget all about his unsatisfactory, ill-timed proposal, and carry on as if nothing at all had changed between them. How in the world would she manage that?

SADIE CURLED UP in the wide, cushy seat of Adam Sanford's airplane and rested her head against Cassie's shoulder. Last week was the first time she'd ever flown. Now she'd made two trips in two weeks! She'd have to go on the Internet and find out how many miles she'd flown and start writing them down in her journal.

The noise from the plane engines rumbled in her ears and in her belly, but it was kind of a nice feeling. It made her feel sleepy and warm. In the other seats people were talking or tapping away at their laptop keyboards or looking out the windows. She wasn't, though. There were thunderclouds out there, and she could see lightning. That made her nervous, so she kept her eyes closed.

She heard Cassie sigh and slid her hand into her friend's. Cassie was sad about something, and Sadie thought she knew what it was. It had happened last night after she went to bed. Her dad and Cassie had been talking real low and quiet. She'd gotten up to get a drink of water because the hot dogs and s'mores had made her thirsty and the door that closed off her little room had been open just a tiny bit, so she'd peeked out through the crack. What she saw made her forget all about getting a drink of water.

Her dad was kissing Cassie!

Even now a whole day later she could feel the prickles of weirdness it had sent up and down her arms. She'd never seen her dad kiss anyone before.

She didn't want to be sneaky, but it'd been hard to look away. Her dad had stopped kissing Cassie right then, though. He touched her hair, smoothing it gently with his hand the way he did Sadie's sometimes, and then they touched their foreheads together and just stayed that way for a while. The weird prickles had changed to a warm glow inside her and left her feeling as though it was Christmas and her birthday and the Fourth of July all rolled into one.

Grown-ups in love kissed each other for a long time that way, everyone knew that. She'd grinned real wide and had to put her hand over her mouth to keep from giggling with excitement. Her dad and Cassie were falling in love just like in a story or a movie. And if they were in love, they would get married and all three of them would be a family.

Sadie had forgotten all about getting a drink. She'd crawled back into her bed, wrapped her arms around her middle and hugged her happiness close. She'd fallen asleep that way and had a wonderful dream. It was all kind of fuzzy now, but she remembered holding a puppy in her arms—her own puppy—not Puddles, and there was a pony eating grass at the bottom of the hill. And they were going to have a party with Grandma and Grandpa and Lelah and Mia all coming to make ice cream just like they did in the *Little House* books she loved to read. But then, right in the middle of her happy dream, something had awakened her for the second time.

It was Cassie, crying very softly, as if her heart would break.

Sadie opened her eyes despite the lightning flashes outside the window and looked at Cassie's face. She wasn't crying now, but she looked sad. Sadie felt sad, too. She must have gotten it all mixed up. If her dad and Cassie were in love, Cassie wouldn't have cried herself to sleep last night or look so sad now.

Sadie's stomach hurt a little and that was never a good sign. She had the terrible feeling her wish for Cassie to join her family wasn't going to come true, after all.

CHAPTER FOURTEEN

"NOTHING NEW on the Gina Grosso–watch blogs," Mia announced, sounding a little disappointed. "No one's posted a reply to the last entry for the past three days."

"I'm sorry, what did you say? I wasn't paying attention," Cassie murmured. Her thoughts were far removed from their small kitchen, even further removed from the mystery of Dean and Patsy Grosso's long-lost child, which preoccupied her mother and sister's spare time these days.

"No problem," Mia said. "The weekend's probably catching up with you. I'd be tired, too, if I'd spent the last four days the way you have," she finished with a touch of envy. The sisters were alone in their little kitchen. It was almost midnight and Lelah had gone to bed two hours earlier, just after Cassie got home from the airport with Sadie. Ethan's daughter was asleep, too, on their living-room couch. The thunderstorms she had seen from the plane had closed in on Talladega, and it would be the middle of the night before the team's charter flight with Ethan on board landed in Charlotte.

"I am tired," Cassie admitted. "You were talking about Gina Grosso?"

"I said there haven't been any new theories on who

Gina Grosso might be, or even any new hints from the blogger—whoever that is."

"Probably some guy with no social skills, holed up in his parents' basement watching all the sports and gossip networks and listening to satellite radio."

Mia wrinkled her forehead. "That's pretty harsh. The latest theory is that the infant Gina didn't die in Mexico where the kidnappers supposedly took her all those years ago. The blogger's convinced she's somewhere in the Charlotte area and possibly even connected to NASCAR in some way. I mean, isn't that just too spooky? It gives me goose bumps just thinking about it."

All these years of not knowing—how had Patsy and Dean Grosso borne it? Such a loss must weigh heavily on their minds. Yet when she'd met the Grossos, Dean and Patsy and Juliana and Milo, and renewed her acquaintance with Sophia, they had all seemed happy. It gave her hope that she could live her own life free of the nightmares of the past.

"And it's possible she's been living right around here all along." Mia was still talking. "It's all so mysterious. I know for a fact the newspapers and probably the police are trying to track down whoever it is who's writing the blog. He must know *something* he's not telling."

"Maybe it's not a *guy* in his basement. Maybe it's a girl," Cassie said absently, still only giving half her attention to her sister. "No one knows who's posting this stuff, do they?"

"No. Whoever it is is covering his—or her—tracks pretty well. And it doesn't have to be some geeky computer genius, either. Ernie says it's easier than you think to be able to hide your IP address and reroute your posts through anonymous servers, all kinds of ways."

Cassie smiled, despite her lingering heartache. Mia couldn't have a conversation about anything these days, including the weather, without peppering it with quotes and observations from Sanford Racing's chief mechanic.

"But I would sure like to know who's behind this whole thing." Mia fell silent, the only sound in the room the tapping of her keyboard and the laboring of the refrigerator motor.

"No news on the Alan Cargill murder, either, on the *Observer* site," she said a minute or two later. "Ernie was talking about him a little at the shop the other day. About how it was such a shame he was killed just as he was retiring and selling the team to the Grossos, that whoever the murderer is he's nothing but a dirty rotten coward to stab an old man to death that way. Ernie knew Alan from way back when Cargill gave a lot of people their start in NASCAR—people like Dean Grosso, Shakey Paulson, even Ethan Hunt. Did you know that?"

"No, I didn't know." And she wasn't likely to learn those kinds of details about his past from Ethan himself, not after what had happened between them Saturday night.

"That New York detective, what's his name, Lucas Hayes or Haines or something like that who's working on the murder investigation, is back in town interviewing more people, according to this article. You'd think he's talked to everyone who might know anything already, wouldn't you? I mean, it's been five months since the murder."

"Maybe he has new clues," Cassie said, trying to keep her mind on the conversation instead of obsessively playing the disastrous scene in the motor home with Ethan over and over in her head.

"Maybe?" Mia sounded doubtful. "My sources tell me the investigation's hit a dead end."

"Your sources?" That made Cassie forget momentarily the pain circling her heart.

Mia colored prettily. Cassie couldn't help but notice how happy she looked. She had turned from a pretty girl into a woman overnight, it seemed. She loved her job. She loved everything about working for Sanford Racing. "What sources?"

"I shouldn't have said 'sources,'" Mia replied. "I was just getting into the *CSI* thing. Don't worry, Cassie. I'm not running off at the mouth. And no one's telling me anything they shouldn't. You don't last long in a shop Ethan Hunt runs if you've got a motor mouth. I get most of the stuff I've heard off the Internet and the newspapers. After a while you can sort out what's for real and what's not."

"I know you're conscientious, but be careful who you talk to," Cassie warned, echoing Ethan's advice to her. She resumed staring out the kitchen window into the backyard, pretending to keep an eye on Puddles, silhouetted by a security light above their neighbor's garage as he made his evening rounds of every bush and tree in their small fenced-in yard. "I'll let Puddles inside and then I'm going to bed."

"Mmm," Mia said, her attention once more focused on the laptop screen.

Cassie opened the back door and whistled for the Yorkie. How was she ever going to face Ethan tomorrow and go on as if nothing had happened between them? The more she thought about it, the more she realized it had to have been the kiss that threw her for such a loop. It had caught her by surprise. It had been seismic. It had curled her toes and stolen her breath and left her trembling with desire and aching for all the things she'd always told herself were silly romantic claptrap and unbecoming a United States Marine.

Even now the memory of the kiss conjured up visions of white lace and wedding veils and rose petals thrown by little girls in ruffled white dresses as she glided down a church aisle—toward a handsome man who would love, honor and cherish her.

The kiss had stolen her common sense and her ability to make a rational decision. Instead of explaining herself like an intelligent human being after he made his perfectly reasonable proposal of marriage, she'd behaved like an utter romantic twit. She'd turned him down.

She should have had the courage to say yes. She should have had the courage to take what he offered and work toward the happily-ever-after.

"Cassie, come look! You're mentioned in one of the racing blogs."

Cassie felt as if a mortar round had gone off under her feet. "What are you talking about?" she demanded, shooing Puddles in and practically shutting the door on his stub of a tail. "Let me see." Cassie skirted the kitchen table and peered over Mia's shoulder.

"Look—right here," Mia said, pointing. "This guy's a part-time reporter for some of the racing magazines. Internet stuff mostly but he has his own blog, too. I've been reading him for a year or so." She kept on reading as she talked, her eyes getting rounder with each sweep of the screen. "Wow!"

"What?" Cassie forgot all about going to bed. She sat down beside her sister. "What does it say?"

Mia turned her head and gave Cassie a long look. "What were you up to down there in Talladega?" she asked.

"Watching over Sadie, what do you think I was doing?" Cassie snapped. *Coming close to having my heart broken,* she thought, but didn't say.

"Well, according to the *Racing Scoop* blog, you were not only mixed up in an altercation with reporters, you were seen more than once with...Trey Sanford!" Mia seemed to freeze with her finger above the touch pad. "And Ethan Hunt!"

"Let me see that." Cassie reached over and pulled the laptop in front of her. It took a moment for her to calm her breathing enough to focus on the words on the screen. A picture of the guy she'd confronted in front of the Sanford hauler stared back at her from a corner of the screen. She read the story in horror:

Posted: 12:38 p.m. CST

I was among a group of reporters outside the Sanford Racing team hauler after the NASCAR Nationwide Series race at 'Dega on Saturday. Seems bad boy driver Trey Sanford has given up racking up frequent flyer miles with trips to Mexico—at least for the time being—and turned in a couple of excellent driving performances.

Okay, so you can read about the Mexico trips half a dozen other places in the blogosphere, but here's an EXCLUSIVE!!! you're going to find nowhere else but here. Seems our boy Trey isn't content with occasional midnight trysts with beautiful women in Mexico. This weekend he was seen around the track with another looker, Crew Chief Ethan Hunt's daughter Sadie's new nanny. Couldn't track down the lady's name, but she can sure put the hurt on a guy. Literally. Easy on the eyes, sure, but don't be fooled—the lady knows her stuff when it comes to self-defense. But don't take my word for it—ask Ashley Bainer's cameraman.

That didn't stop NASCAR's more reticent crew chief from turning protective of his special ladies, though. When he gave me that famous scowl of his and barked, "No comment," I took myself off in a hurry.

All the late-night flights and reporter scrums didn't hurt Trey's racing any. He won the NASCAR Nationwide race on Saturday when he strapped himself into the seat in place of the ailing Shelley Green, then repeated the win Sunday in the NASCAR Sprint Cup Series car, finishing seven-tenths of a second ahead of Justin Murphy to bring home his first win since the Shootout at Daytona.

Way to go, Trey!

But can his good luck carry over to the race next Sunday? Short track has never been Trey's strong point. I think I'll spend my time between races trying to get more scoop on the nanny with the attitude. Maybe she was the key to Trey's good driving this week. Could be three's a charm. Three charming ladies, that is, although rumor has it that Trey and model girlfriend Becky Peters have called it quits for good this time. Good to see Wild Bobby's baby boy and the Sanford Racing team back.

"Oh, Lord," Cassie said, and put her head in her hands. "How did you find the time to start up a thing with Trey out there?" Mia asked, taking back her laptop. Cassie didn't try to stop her. Her arms felt like lead weights attached to her shoulders, too heavy to do her bidding.

"Are there more of those kinds of posts waiting to jump out and bite me?" she asked, her stomach tying itself in knots.

"I don't know. I suppose I could Google your name and see."

"Do it, please." She stood up, too nervous to sit and wait. She tiptoed into the living room. Puddles had hopped onto the couch and was sleeping curled against Sadie's side. They were going to have pancakes for breakfast tomorrow. She couldn't forget to remind Mia.

She walked back into the kitchen. Mia looked up from the keyboard. "I don't understand. I mean, you were staying with Mom and Sadie and our little peeing machine in a motor home one weekend, and with Sadie the other. I don't care how luxurious some of them are, there's not that much room in them. Hanky-panky-wise, I mean."

"There was no hanky-panky—you know me better than that." Might as well tell Mia the truth. Mia wouldn't let her rest until she got it. "I did meet Trey, at the Phoenix race, to be precise. And this weekend I was mixed up in an altercation with a bunch of reporters, but that's all there was to it. Did you find anything else about it?"

"Nope," Mia said, shutting the lid. "That entry was it."

"Thank God. I'm going to bed."

"Wait a minute. Is he still seeing that model or did they break up like the blog said? Did he sneak off to Mexico again while you were in Alabama? Did he put the moves on you?" Mia demanded.

"I don't know the answers to the first two questions. And

it's none of your business what did or didn't happen between me and him." She walked out of the kitchen without a backward glance. "G'night. Don't forget to turn out the lights."

But Mia had the last word. "Okay, Trey didn't make any moves on you. But that wasn't the only guy the blogger mentioned. What about Ethan?"

CASSIE LOOKED around the kitchen table. It was a dreary, rainy Monday morning, which exactly matched her mood. But with the exception of her mother's pink nose and dark circles under her eyes from her lingering cold, the other faces at the table were perky and full of energy. She, on the other hand, felt as if she hadn't slept a wink all night. And she hadn't.

"How's your cold this morning, Mom?" Cassie asked as Mia, the designated pancake maker in the household, presided over the countertop griddle.

"Better," Lelah said, spearing a bite of pancake with her fork, one with a large, padded handle that was easier for her to grasp. "I slept really well last night. I think I'll stay home today, if you don't mind, though."

"I'm staying home today, too," Cassie informed her. "I talked to Ethan earlier this morning. He and Sadie will be spending the afternoon with his sister and his father." It had been a short conversation, a little stilted, but actually not as awkward as she thought it would be, but in a way more painful. He sounded as though she was just another casual friend, just the nanny. True, that was what she'd told him she wanted, but still it hurt and she was relieved not to have to face him in person again so soon.

"I'm going to play with my cousins," Sadie informed them around a mouthful of pancake. "They've got a day off school for spring teachers' conferences and Dad said I could spend time with them and give Cassie a break. Do you need a break from me?" she asked, frowning a bit.

"No, I do not need a break from you," Cassie said, making a funny face for Sadie's amusement.

"You should have fun today." Lelah gave Sadie a smile and pushed the syrup bottle closer to her plate.

The girl shrugged. "I probably will. Aunt Grace always thinks of cool things to do. Thanks." Her pancakes were already swimming in syrup, but she added more. "What are you going to do?" she asked, including all of them in the question, but looking at Cassie.

"I'm going to give myself a manicure," Mia said, sliding onto her chair with a plateful of pancakes. "Ernie had me working on one of Shelley Green's engines last week, and my nails are a disaster." She didn't sound upset about it, though.

"I'm doing laundry," Cassie said.

"Dad and I have laundry to do, too."

"I'll help you with it tomorrow," Cassie said, and was rewarded with a smile.

"Tomorrow. Yeah, we can do it together tomorrow."

The phone rang. Mia reached behind her and plucked the old-fashioned green wall phone off its cradle. "Connors residence," she mumbled, swallowing the last of a bite of pancake, then snapped to attention the way a Marine recruit did when the drill instructor showed up. "Yes. She's here. Just a moment, please. I'll get her." She held out the phone, covering the receiver with her hand so that whoever was on the other end couldn't hear. "It's the guy you just met but didn't do anything else with," she hissed, looking more than a little impressed and a lot curious. "Trey Sanford!"

"Trey?"

"In the flesh. Or at least on the phone. Talk to him, Sarge," Mia commanded, "and be nice to him. His brother holds my future success in NASCAR in his hands."

"Hello?" Cassie rolled her eyes in response to Mia's dramatics.

"Hi, it's Trey," the familiar sexy voice replied. "I got your number from Ethan when I phoned him a few minutes ago."

"Oh," Cassie said, wishing he'd just taken the time to look up her number in the book, instead. "What can I do for you?"

"I'm going to put on a little celebration party for the team Wednesday afternoon. Nothing fancy, just a thank-you to let them know I appreciate everyone working so hard for my two wins this past weekend."

"That's very generous of you," she said. Sanford Racing wasn't as big as some of the juggernaut four-car teams, but there were still quite a number of people employed there. He wasn't talking a sack of deli sandwiches and a couple of six-packs of beer, either, no matter how casually he spoke. "I'm afraid I'll have to take a rain check, though. I…I have plans for Wednesday."

"Like what?" he said, apparently not the least put off by her vague refusal. "You mean besides taking care of Sadie?"

"Well—"

"I want you to bring your mother, too."

"My mother?"

"We met at Phoenix, remember? Your sister can get the

directions to our place from Ernie. He's got all the details. I'll expect y'all around four. Dress casual."

It was time to take the upper hand. Gratitude to Ethan for giving Mia her chance in NASCAR was as far as her obligation to Sanford Racing went. "I'm honored you thought to invite—"

"Uh-oh. Sounds like another turndown coming. Look, Cassie, I feel bad about what happened at Phoenix and Talladega. Getting caught up in my media scrambles isn't the best intro to NASCAR you can have. Come to the party. Meet the rest of the team and my mother. You'll like her. Let me make it up to you."

"It's not necessary, really." Another situation where she'd be thrown into Ethan's company. The thought tied her stomach in knots. How was she ever going to feel comfortable around him again?

"Yes, it is necessary. It's either that or I start asking you out to dinner again. I promise you'll have a great time."

Cassie looked over her shoulder and saw her mother and her sister exchange excited, quizzical looks. Sadie was the only one not paying attention to the phone call. She was still eating, sneaking bites of pancake to Puddles under the table when she thought no one was looking. Cassie felt her resolve begin to crumble. She didn't want to play the heavy. She'd made a bargain with the devil, her own heart, when she agreed to remain as Sadie's nanny after rejecting Sadie's father. "All right," she said, surrendering with as much grace as she could muster. "Thanks for inviting us. We'll be there."

CHAPTER FIFTEEN

"HE'S GOT A LOT BETTER opinion of my influence on the Connors women than I do." Ethan scowled down at the screen of his cell phone and snapped it shut with more force than necessary.

"What are you talking about?" Grace asked.

"Trey's making sure I'm on board with his plan to bring all the Connors women with us to Richmond."

"What are you talking about? You've never let anyone con you into anything, especially not Trey Sanford."

Ethan and Grace were momentarily alone in his dad's kitchen. It was a big square room that took up most of the back of the four-bedroom colonial where the Hunt brood had all grown up. Dan and Grace's mother-in-law, Susan Winters, were sitting outside on the patio watching Grace's three kids and Sadie play in the big fenced-in backyard while Grace prepared supper for all of them.

"Trey says he doesn't know what kind of magic having Sadie, Cassie and her mom, Lelah—and that damned dog of theirs—at Phoenix and 'Dega produced, but he says it was powerful stuff and he wants it there for him at Richmond, too."

"Well," Grace said with maddening matter-of-factness,

"he's a stock car driver. They might not be the most superstitious men on earth, but I'd be hard-pressed to tell you who *are*."

"Hell, I don't care a lick about what little jujus my driver needs to feel comfortable in his seat, but I object to being manipulated by his quirks. Cassie working magic, that's a good one," he snorted, and immediately regretted his words because Grace picked up on them instantly.

She cocked her head and gave him a long, considering look. "Cassie? I assumed you'd be more upset about him manipulating your *daughter,* not her nanny."

"I'm always thinking about Sadie's welfare," he said, "but Trey's a step ahead of me there, too. I've had Sadie with me for the last two races. Richmond's a hop, skip and jump away from here compared to Phoenix, or even 'Dega. What excuse do I have for leaving her at home this weekend? She's still on spring break, and Ford and Martha are still on their cruise."

"What are you going to do?" she asked, moving one of the roasted red pepper mousse appetizers she'd been arranging on a plate for the four of them just a fraction of an inch to complete the presentation—the kids were getting cream cheese and strawberry jam, and they looked darned good, too. Grace was a perfectionist. Even little snacks for family and friends were treated as though they were being offered to her A-list clients.

"I guess I'll go along with it," he said wearily. "If Trey thinks it was the Connors women and Sadie who brought him a top-five finish and two wins in a row, who am I to say it wasn't?"

Grace wrapped her arms around his neck and gave him

a quick hug. "Only the genius crew chief who engineered the winning race strategies without any help from magic nannies and their mothers."

"Yeah, if I'm that good, why am I thinking that maybe he's not *that* far out in left field?" Ethan propped his elbows on the table and rested his chin on his hands.

"Will Cassie and her mother go along with such a hare-brained assumption?" Grace asked, leaning back against the counter.

"Cassie will never stand for it," he said flatly. "I can guarantee you that. She's not the superstitious type."

"I wouldn't know," she said pointedly. "We've never met."

"She's only been Sadie's nanny for two weeks."

"You'd never know that from listening to Sadie talk. Cassie this and Cassie that. She's grown very attached to this woman in a very short period of time."

Sadie's not the only one, Ethan thought.

Grace waited a few moments for his response. When he didn't say anything she handed him a canapé. "You know, if you change your mind she's welcome to stay with me next weekend. I only have two parties to cater and they're both local." She lifted her arms above her head and stretched. "Practically a vacation," she said with a wry smile.

"Then that settles it," Ethan said. "You spend time with your kids and I'll…let mine be turned into a good luck charm for an unfocused playboy."

Grace shook her head and rolled her eyes. "Quit being so hard on yourself. Trey's maybe not as disciplined as some other drivers, Kent Grosso, or even Justin Murphy, but he's got grit and he's got the breeding. He just needs someone to set him on the straight and narrow. You'll talk sense into him before Sunday, I guarantee it. They don't call you the toughest chief in NASCAR without a reason."

He grunted. "Among other things."

She laughed. "Granted, having Sadie proclaimed a good luck charm is unconventional, but it's not going to spoil her—she's too grounded for that—and you have to admit that being in the thick of things is a thrill for her. She's making new friends, growing up right in front of our eyes. Don't spoil it for her, or for yourself. Especially since you seem to have found a jewel in her nanny."

"Friend," Ethan replied automatically. "Sadie's too old for a nanny as she's probably already told you."

Grace smiled as she turned back to her task. "From what Sadie told me about the episode with the reporter, Cassie Connors is a good *friend* to have around."

"She is."

"What about you? Is she your friend, too?"

"Yes, she is."

"Could she be more than a friend?"

"Grace—"

She held up a hand, silencing him for a moment. "I'm asking for Sadie's sake. She needs a woman in her life, Ethan. So do you. Laura's been gone eight years. It's time to move on."

He could confide in Grace. They'd always been close, had shared a lot of confidences over the years. They both had lost their first loves, the partners they'd expected to grow old with. She would hear him out and help him figure out what to do about Cassie and the role he wanted her to play in his life. But before he could form his thoughts into coherent speech, a quartet of laughing, noisy kids tumbled through the door from the backyard, followed by his father and Susan.

"We'll talk later," she mouthed. She turned to the older couple. "Mosquitoes finally drive you inside? Snacks are ready. I thought we could have a cocktail to toast Ethan's win at Talladega."

Susan glanced at the clock on the microwave above the stove. Grace's mother-in-law was a couple of years younger than Dan, just shy of sixty, medium height and weight, with brown eyes and brown hair untouched by gray. The Hunts and Winterses had been neighbors for decades. Ethan had spent as much time in Susan's home when he was a boy as he had in his own. "Good heavens, look at the time. I'm late. I'm moderating a discussion on my quilting group's Internet forum at seven." She fluttered her hands in his direction. "I'm already late. Congratulations again on Trey's win at Talladega, Ethan, but I'll have to pass on the cocktail." She looked over the plate of appetizers Grace held up for her inspection. "Oh, but I must try these. Oh, marvelous!" she enthused, smacking her lips. "One more for the road, please. Got to run."

"She's sure spending a lot of time online these days," Grace observed from the window above the sink as her mother-in-law disappeared through the gap in the hedges.

"Nothing wrong with that," Dan said just a shade defensively. "Come to think of it, I need to check my e-mail, too. Call me when dinner's ready." He left the kitchen without eating anything, leaving Grace looking slightly affronted by his lack of interest.

Ethan's father, according to his brother Jared's accounts, had been spending a lot of time in Internet chat rooms, and not all of them were NASCAR-related, either. A great many of them were for singles—and not necessarily senior singles. Ethan hadn't expected his father to mourn his adopted mother for the rest of his life, but he hadn't expected him to be looking for companionship quite so soon.

Grace's son went straight for the plate of crackers and jam. Sadie and the girls followed a bit more sedately.

"These look really good, Aunt Grace," Sadie said, popping one into her mouth. "Mmm, yummy."

"I'm glad you like them, honey."

"Could you give me the recipe? Cassie and I could make them at our house one day. It'd be fun."

"Sure. I'll type it up for you after dinner."

"Thanks. Cassie likes to cook, doesn't she, Dad?"

"Uh, yeah, Cassie's a good cook."

Grace raised her eyebrows at him but didn't comment further. "Why don't you guys go into the den and watch TV while I get dinner on the table?"

"Okay." Fifteen seconds later they were stampeding out of the kitchen into Dan's sanctuary, arguing noisily about which show to watch.

"That'll get Dad off the computer," Grace said, grinning, pouring glasses of iced tea for the two of them.

"You are a devious woman," he said, saluting her with his glass.

His sister's plan worked perfectly. Five minutes after being invaded by his grandkids, Dan returned to the kitchen. "Can't hear myself think in there," he grumbled. "What do we have here?" he asked, eyeing the plate of appetizers with more interest this time.

"A couple of new recipes I'm auditioning. Try this roasted red pepper mousse. I think you'll like it."

Dan popped one in his mouth. He chewed and swallowed. "Delicious, Grace. You've got a winner here."

"Excellent. You're my target audience, you know. I'm making these for the county Veterans of Foreign Wars conference."

"They'll be a hit," Dan decreed.

"What about the salmon pâté?" She was making more strawberry jam and cream cheese crackers to replenish the plate the kids had emptied in about ten seconds flat.

Dan gave her a thumbs-up. "Top-notch."

"How was your weekend?" she asked as she worked.

"Lucas Haines, that New York detective, came to see me Friday afternoon," Dan said.

"What?" Grace glanced at Ethan, a tiny furrow etched between her eyebrows. "You never said anything about Lucas Haines wanting to interview you." Grace had catered the affair at the swank New York hotel the night of Alan Cargill's murder, and her encounters with Lucas Haines had been more frequent and prolonged than Ethan's.

"What could you possibly tell the guy, Dad? You were here, a thousand miles away from where it happened." Champions Week and the NASCAR Awards Banquet had taken place only a couple of weeks after Linda's death, and Dan had had no interest in attending. Ethan had only gone to New York because Adam expected it of him. There were sponsors to meet and stroke, and so he'd had to put his sorrow at Linda's death aside and make the trip.

"He's evidently trying to get some insight into Alan's friends and business dealings," Dan explained. "Came over Friday afternoon. Sat right there in the same chair Ethan's sitting in. Wouldn't take a beer or a cup of coffee, even. All business, that one."

"But I thought the police believe it was a random mugging. A crime of opportunity, don't they call it?" Grace asked. "Alan was just in the wrong place at the wrong time."

"That's what I thought, too," Dan said, looking grim. "Lucas Haines is a hard guy to read. He asks a lot of questions, but he doesn't return the favor."

Ethan had had the same impression when he met the New York detective the day after Alan's death. The interview had lasted approximately two minutes. Just long enough for Ethan, like dozens of others who had attended the banquet in the hotel, to verify that he had been nowhere near the service hallway where the murder had taken place and that he had various witnesses to prove it. He'd been impressed with the detective's professional attitude and insightful questions but he had no useful information to give the man and had put the encounter out of his mind once the new race season began in earnest.

"He's a smart guy, but you can't make a murder case out of nothing. I couldn't tell him anything about what Alan was planning to do in New York. I hadn't seen him since Linda's funeral. The only thing I could tell the guy was that I was damned sorry I didn't have a chance to say goodbye to a man I knew and respected for forty years. I sure hope they catch the sorry bastard who killed him, but it won't be because I had anything helpful to add to the investigation."

"I don't want to have to talk to him again if it isn't necessary," Grace said with a shudder. "I want to forget that awful night. When I think how close all of us were to a maniac with a knife…well, I just don't want to think about it anymore."

"Before he left he asked me if I knew anything about the Gina Grosso kidnapping," Dan revealed.

"Whatever for? He can't believe the murder and the kidnapping were connected in any way?"

Ethan agreed with his sister. It didn't make sense that the detective was interested in the decades-old kidnapping. There was no connection to the Cargill murder as far as he could see. How could there be? Perhaps Haines was just curious like anyone else. That didn't bother Ethan. It just made the guy seem more human.

"That one stumped me, too. I told him you boys and me were living in Indiana then. I was crew chief for an Indy car team. Didn't have anything to do with stock car racing. Open wheel all the way, in those days. I never knew anything about Dean and Patsy Grosso's baby being kidnapped. Never heard a word about it all the years I spent in NASCAR, for that matter.

"Could have knocked me over with a feather when the story came out. Said he was just curious, that's all. Took his fancy, I suppose, because of all the time he's spending around racing these days. He shook my hand, thanked me for my time and left." Dan pushed his chair away from the table and stood up. "I think I'll go spend some time on the Internet," he said. "There's nothing much on TV tonight, anyway, and maybe Hope answered my last e-mail."

"Tell her I said hi," Grace said, raising her voice to carry over to the kids who had begun to argue among themselves. "I know I owe her a phone call but she's never there to take it." Their baby sister, Hope, Dan and Linda's child together, was an industrial psychologist, a "team builder" in her own words. She lived in Dallas, the only one of his siblings to have strayed far from their North Carolina roots. Hope had an impressive track record in her chosen field and on bad days Ethan seriously considered hiring her himself to get his rough-edged team to work together.

"E-mail my foot. I bet Dad's headed for those singles chat rooms Susan got him hooked on," Grace said, her frown returning. "I don't know if he's ready for a new relationship yet."

"That's probably why he's sticking to the chat rooms. He doesn't have to follow through on any conversation if he doesn't want to."

Grace raised an inquisitive eyebrow in Ethan's direction, and he hurriedly changed the subject, having thought better about confiding his own problems to his sister. "Why do you think Lucas Haines was asking Dad about the Gina Grosso kidnapping?"

"I haven't a clue," she said. "Probably just curious, like he said. It's a compelling story. Dean and Patsy keeping a secret like that for so many years, not even telling Sophia or Kent about their sister. And with Gina being Kent's twin, it must be doubly hard on him."

Ethan wasn't that well acquainted with Dean and Patsy's son. Kent was a few years younger than he was—Grace's age, if he remembered correctly.

Grace went quiet for a moment, her hands stilled at their task. "What do you think of all these rumors about the kidnapping flying around the Internet? Susan talks about it all the time when the kids and I are over there. It's kind of an obsession with her."

"I haven't paid a lot of attention to it. I've had too much on my plate to speculate on who the long-lost Gina might be. Heck, she could be any one of half a dozen women I know." Becky Peters had Trey convinced she could be Gina one night when we were all sitting around the hauler. Right hair. Right blood type—

"Right age," Grace said archly.

"She's twenty-seven."

"On her résumé, maybe." Grace grinned, wiggling her eyebrows.

"No kidding? Had me fooled." A thought struck him. "You could even be her." He started ticking off points on his fingers. "You're the right age."

"I'm four months older than Kent Grosso. Gina was his twin, remember."

"What's your blood type?"

"B positive."

"Same as the baby's, right?" he said. One of the newspaper accounts he'd read last winter had mentioned the blood type and somehow he'd remembered it.

"It's a very common blood type." She waved off that argument with a flick of her hand.

"You're blond. I think the Grosso baby was, too. Sophia is."

"Sophia gets help from a very talented stylist," Grace said, making a purring sound. "Mine's natural."

"The blog everyone's reading says Gina's connected to NASCAR. You're connected to NASCAR."

"Tenuously."

"Hey, I'm just stating the facts, ma'am."

"I'm not Gina Grosso," she said with finality, then grew serious all of a sudden. "But as a mother I don't know how Patsy and Dean have lived with not knowing what happened to their baby all these years. No wonder they never talked about it to anyone. Do you think of your real mother often?" she surprised him by asking.

Ethan felt something in him tighten slightly. He seldom talked of his and Jared's mother. She had died when he was so little his memories were faint and fragmentary. "Yes, sometimes."

Grace sat down beside him and rested her hand on his. It was quiet in the kitchen, but they could both hear the kids bickering again in the den and knew they didn't have much more time to themselves. "I think about my father, too," she admitted. "All Mom told me about him was that he loved to race cars. And he was the proudest man in the world the day I was born. That's not much to remember him by."

"Did you ever want to get in touch with his people?" Ethan asked. He and Jared had spent summer vacations with his maternal grandparents, stayed close until their deaths, only six months apart, a few years earlier, but his stepmom, Linda, had had no family of her own, and he never recalled her speaking of Grace's father at all.

"I've never tried. I don't want to upset Dad by going off looking for a family I've never known. *You're* my family," she said, leaning forward to give him a quick peck on the cheek. "All of you. Dad and Jared and Hope, and you, big brother, are the only family I've ever known. The only family I'll ever want."

CHAPTER SIXTEEN

"OMIGOD! THIS IS the biggest house I've ever seen." Mia craned her neck to look out the windshield of Cassie's car as they approached Trey and Adam Sanford's family home. It was an impressive building, Cassie conceded, all mellow brick and stone with dormer windows beneath a gabled roof. You couldn't see Lake Norman, the huge impound lake north of Charlotte where many NASCAR luminaries resided, but she would be surprised if the mansion didn't have access to the lakeshore. The grounds were beautifully landscaped and the flowerbeds were bursting with spring color.

"It's lovely," Lelah breathed from the front passenger seat. She tightened her grip on her straw purse, and her smile was almost as big as Mia's. "I can't believe a couple of weeks ago I was wondering if we were going to get the grocery budget to stretch to the end of the month without having mac and cheese twice a week, and now I've not only spent the weekend in Phoenix, seen a NASCAR race—or heard one, anyway—and been entertained by Milo and Juliana Grosso, but now I'm attending a party given by Kath Sanford and her sons. Someone pinch me—I must be dreaming."

Mia reached across the seat and gave her mother a tiny

pinch on her arm. "Ouch," Lelah squeaked. "What did you do that for?"

"You just told me to—" Mia giggled "—and just to make sure we're not having the same awesome dream I pinched myself, too."

"What about you, Cassie? Doesn't this all seem like a dream come true?"

"It's like a dream all right." And not a very happy one at the moment, she added to herself.

"I wonder if Grace Winters is catering the party. She caters all the best NASCAR parties, you know," Mia said, smug in her insider knowledge.

"I imagine you can find out if you go snooping around the kitchen entrance to see whose catering truck is parked there."

"I hope you have better manners than that," Lelah said.

"Don't worry, I won't be that gauche." Mia's arm shot between them, pointing out the window. "Hey, there's a parking space."

Cassie jockeyed her small car into the barely adequate opening between two big 4x4s. When she turned off the ignition she looked up to find Trey and his brother watching her maneuver with approval.

"Nice work," Trey said, opening the door for her while Adam circled the car to perform the same service for Lelah.

"The big boss! Don't let me do anything stupid," Mia hissed in her ear.

"You'll be fine," Cassie whispered as she felt around on the floor for her handbag.

"How do I look? Is this outfit okay?" Mia asked. "Maybe I should have just worn my uniform. Some of the other guys are and I don't want to look too girly." She bit her lip and cast a glance down at her stretchy short-sleeved knit top and cropped pants. Ernie Markham had sent Mia home from the shop an hour early to give her time to prepare for her first official "office party."

"You look fine. As a matter of fact, you look terrific. Stop worrying and enjoy."

"Okay," Mia mouthed soundlessly as Adam Sanford opened the passenger door and greeted Lelah warmly.

Cassie took advantage of the small diversion. She looked over her shoulder and whispered to Mia, "Stand up straight. Shake his hand, look him in the eye and smile. You've got a smile that'd melt steel."

Mia tested out her smile. "Oorah, Sarge."

"Oorah."

"Cassie, Lelah. Glad you could make it."

"Hello, Trey," Cassie said, pretending she didn't see his hand as she exited the car unassisted.

"Always the independent one, aren't you?"

"Yes."

He gave her a knowing grin, not one bit daunted by her response, opened the rear door for Mia and helped her out of the car. "Hello, Mia. Welcome."

"Thanks, Trey."

"Adam, I'd like you to meet Cassie and Mia's mother. Mrs. Connors, my big brother, Adam."

"Please, call me Lelah. Thank you so much for inviting us today." Her mother was beaming. How long had it been, Cassie wondered, since she'd received such courteous treatment from two handsome men?

"Lelah, it's a pleasure to meet you," Adam said, taking

her ruined hand gently in his. "Mia," he said, smiling from the far side of the car.

"Mr. Sanford," she said, smiling back.

"Let's go inside so that I can introduce you to our mother." Adam offered Lelah his arm as they moved from the pavement to the brick walkway. Trey fell into step beside Cassie. Moments later they were ushered into a house as imposing and luxurious on the inside as it was on the outside, but once she'd adjusted to the opulence, Cassie realized it was a home and not just a showplace.

People, singly and in couples, some still wearing their dark blue Sanford Racing shirts and khakis, others in casual dress, roamed through the soaring foyer and in and out of a formally decorated dining room carrying plates of food and drinks in tall glasses, all talking discreetly and some not so discreetly, gawking at their employer's residence, everyone seeming to enjoy themselves. Cassie caught a glimpse of a more masculine den and library on the other side of the wide hallway as they were led into a huge kitchen where Kath Sanford, a handsome woman in her sixties, presided over a buffet of food and drinks tended by a trio of caterers in starched white shirts and black slacks.

As Cassie had suspected when Trey issued his invitation to the party, it was far more than just beer and deli trays. There were all kinds of beautifully arranged appetizers and salads and platters of small sandwiches and desserts, as well as chips and dips and veggie trays clearly designed to please the children in attendance.

Once more Trey made the introductions after Adam excused himself to greet another group of newly arrived guests.

"Trey told me about y'all," Kath Sanford said with a gracious but subdued smile. "And your little dog, too. My son seems quite taken with all of you, and with Ethan's daughter, Sadie, as well. Although, I don't subscribe to his theory that you're responsible for his excellent showing at Phoenix and Talladega."

"Sorry?" Cassie said, puzzled by the remark. A shiver ran up and down her arm. What was the woman saying? "Would you mind explaining?"

"Mom's not in the least superstitious," Trey said, "but I am. You and Sadie are my good luck charms, Cassie."

"That's ridiculous," Cassie blurted.

Trey's eyes narrowed. "No, it's not. C'mon, humor me. I want all of you there again at Richmond. Mia included." Behind her Cassie heard her sister suck in her breath. "Ethan's already agreed y'all should be there, too."

He had given his approval of Trey's scheme without consulting her?

In truth they had barely spoken a dozen words since he'd picked Sadie up at the house late Monday morning. The conversations they'd had since were cordial enough, but always centered on Sadie and her needs, nothing personal, nothing about what had passed between them that night in the motor home. Cassie felt her blood pressure rise even as her heart sank into her toes. She had thought, despite their differences, that he had more respect for her than that. "Naturally I'll attend the race with Sadie if Ethan asks me to," Cassie said, choosing her words very carefully, "but we haven't discussed the matter yet."

"As it should be," Kath said, and this time her smile

held real warmth. "You're not the superstitious sort, either, I take it?"

"No, ma'am, I'm not."

"Your regard for Sadie shows both common sense and a sense of duty. I commend you. Rumor has it you came out the winner of an altercation with a less-than-stellar representative of the electronic media at Talladega? Perhaps that's also figuring into my son's insistence on you being there for him at yet another race." This woman might choose not to attend races anymore, but she certainly kept her finger on the pulse of her family's race team.

"I wouldn't know," Cassie replied. "As I said, the matter has not been discussed with me."

"Well, why don't we?" Trey suggested. "I'll round up Ethan and my brother."

"I think that would be a good idea," Cassie agreed, focusing her concentration on her newfound indignation to keep despair at bay.

"Trey, this is a social affair," his mother said in a warning tone.

"We're just going to straighten out a misunderstanding."

"Very well." She gestured toward the buffet table and the bar set up in a corner of the big room. "Make yourself at home, won't you, Mrs. Connors, Cassie. Fill your plates, have a drink. Mia dear, I forgot to welcome you to Sanford Racing. I hope you have a long and successful career with us. Now, if you'll excuse me, I must see to my other guests."

Once Kath Sanford moved off, Trey did likewise, and the three of them were on their own.

"What was that all about?" Mia asked as they made their way to the buffet.

"I'm not sure, but I certainly intend to find out."

"I never expected to be invited to another race," Lelah murmured, picking up a plate from the stack beside an enormous bowl of iced shrimp. "I enjoyed going to Phoenix, but I can't see doing it every week."

"You don't have to go anywhere you don't want to, Mom," Cassie said under her breath as she speared a couple of large shrimp and put them on Lelah's plate.

"Rookie mechanics do not get invited to attend races by their drivers or their owners." Mia smiled and waved her fingers at a couple of her teammates making their way along the other side of the buffet table. She talked to Cassie out of the corner of her mouth. "I'm not going. I don't want to get everyone else in the shop on my case for sucking up to the boss." She looked at Cassie with troubled eyes. "This whole thing is weird. Trey can't really think he won those races just because you and Mom and Sadie were there, can he?"

"Not unless he's mentally deranged," Cassie said, spearing a shrimp with far more force than necessary. "Whatever's wrong with him it must be catching if he's got Ethan convinced, too."

A waiter came by and offered to carry their plates outside. Cassie accepted a glass of wine from one of the servers circulating through the crowd and so did Lelah. Mia took a soda. They skirted the big pool and settled at a table on the patio shaded by a pergola roof covered with honeysuckle vines in orange and pink and yellow. Music played from hidden speakers. People ate and talked, moving from table to table, laughing and animated.

A sixtyish couple stopped by to say hello to Mia and she introduced them as Ernie and Serena Markham. They were on their way to the buffet and promised to return and join them later. "I don't see Ethan or Trey or Adam," Mia said, looking around. "Wonder where they are?"

"Cassie!" She half turned at the sound of her name. It was Sadie, waving from the edge of the patio. She was wearing the outfit they'd chosen earlier in the afternoon before Cassie left to pick up Lelah and Mia for the party, a swingy little skirt and T-shirt in a medley of sherbet colors that complemented the pale gold of her hair. They had bought it on a shopping trip the day before especially for this occasion.

"Hi, Sadie," Cassie said, holding out her arms, aware that several pairs of eyes had turned in their direction as Ethan's daughter greeted her with an exuberant hug. She hugged Sadie back, then gave her a gentle push so that she moved to arm's length. "Let's see. Turn around. I think your new outfit looks great," she said as Sadie spun in a circle.

"I like it, too. Have you seen my dad?"

"Uh, no," Cassie said, stumbling a bit. "Mom and Mia and I only got here a few minutes ago."

"I haven't seen him in a while. I went to the guest house with Tara to see her wedding dress. It's so beautiful! She and Adam are going to get married. I forget exactly when, though. But I'm invited to the wedding—she told me so."

"Great."

"That means I'll need another outfit. We can go shopping again." She waggled her eyebrows and grinned from ear to ear. Sadie had changed so much in the short time they had known each other. Cassie vowed to herself that she would do everything in her power to make sure that transformation continued.

Sadie must be protected. She didn't deserve to be an unwitting pawn in whatever game the Sanford brothers were playing. Good luck charms? Ha! She needed to locate Ethan and make him see the truth as plainly as she did. But it would never do for him to come upon her unawares. If she saw him first, she could deal with the jolt to her senses the first sight of him always produced. She picked up the glass of wine and turned her head to scan the perimeter of the pool.

"There's my dad," Sadie said, pointing. Cassie saw the trio of men moving across the lawn. Adam and Trey were dressed in slacks and open-necked shirts. Ethan was still wearing the dark blue shirt and khakis she'd seen him in earlier in the day. Their clothing might proclaim the difference in their positions at Sanford Racing, but beyond that it was hard to tell who had the most commanding presence.

They stopped for a moment at the edge of the patio. Adam and Ethan exchanged a few words. Trey remained silent but nodded, seeming to agree with whatever they were saying, then turned and walked away from the other two. He caught Cassie watching them and raised his finger to his forehead in a jaunty salute, but there was no laughter in his eyes and his jaw looked set.

Cassie looked down at her glass of wine. She wondered what had just been said. Trey didn't look pleased, but then, how could she really know what he was thinking? He was almost a stranger and a very hard man to read.

When she glanced up again, Ethan was standing beside the table.

"I've been looking for you," he said.

Cassie jumped at the sound of his voice and sloshed

wine over her hand. Her mother and Mia and Sadie were all watching her. What should she do next? The answer was easy. She was a Marine. Attack. Attack. Attack. Never wait for the enemy to come to you. Take the fight to him. "That's a coincidence," she said, standing up so that he didn't tower over her quite so much. "I've been looking for you."

"WE NEED TO TALK," he said. He turned to Lelah and Mia. "Do you mind looking after Sadie for a few minutes? Cassie and I have some things we need to discuss."

"No. She's fine with us. Take your time." Lelah made a shooing motion with her hands. Mia only nodded, looking slightly apprehensive. Sadie looked apprehensive, too.

"Don't be too long," she said. "Okay, Dad? Cassie?"

Sadie had been a little clingy since they'd come home from Alabama. He wondered if she was picking up on the tension between the two of them. She probably was. She was a bright kid. He gave her a reassuring smile. "We won't be long, doodle, I promise."

He put his hand under Cassie's elbow and guided her to a corner of the patio that was out of sight of her family and most of the other guests. When they stopped she whirled around, instantly on the offensive. "What are Trey and his brother up to? What's this silliness about lucky charms and needing me and Sadie and my family at every race? Have you guys lost your senses?"

"Oh, hell," Ethan said. He wished he could get his hands on his driver right then. He'd wring his neck. "I told Trey to let me handle this."

"Handle what? His mother slipped up and mentioned a charade. Smells more like a smokescreen to me. I don't like the fact that my mother and my sister might be involved in it. And Sadie. Most of all Sadie." Her voice broke despite her attempt to appear all calm and collected.

She was worried about Sadie. He hadn't been fooling himself the times he'd thought he'd seen something very much like love shining from her green-gold eyes when she looked at his daughter. No, not something like love. It *was* love. She loved Sadie. She was willing to fight for his daughter's best interests no matter the cost to herself. His own last doubts slipped away. No more tap-dancing around the truth. No more looking for logical reasons for what he was feeling. It was time to go with what his heart was telling him. He loved this woman. That was the beginning and the end of it.

He'd have to put off wooing her until later, though. Right now she looked mad enough to spit nails at him. He jerked his mind back to the problem at hand. What the hell had Trey told her, exactly? "Look, we can't talk here. There are too many people around." He reached down and grabbed her hand. She gave a tug, but he didn't loosen his hold, so she quit struggling.

"Where are we going?" she snapped.

"Just down the hill a little way," he said.

"What's down here?" He could almost see the gears turning in her mind as she assessed the landscape, marking her escape route, the best places to set up defenses, to press an attack. She was in full warrior mode now, and woe to any man she chose to do battle with.

He kept her walking at a fast enough clip to discourage conversation. They marched down the driveway in lockstep, veering off into the woods about halfway down the hill. The lane was narrow and rutted and Cassie had to keep her attention on where she put her feet. A quarter of a mile later the lane ended in a small clearing that Kath Sanford had shown him on an earlier visit to the house.

In the distance Lake Norman glittered in the fading light of the late-April evening. A rustic bench swing hung from a tree branch positioned to take advantage of views of the sunset over the lake. "Have a seat," he said, suiting his own action to his words.

She didn't do as he suggested but took a few more steps closer to the edge of the bluff. "This is a beautiful spot," she allowed.

"It belongs to the Sanfords. Wild Bobby was a womanizer and a real jerk in a lot of other ways, but he realized Lake Norman's potential early on. Bought up a whole lot of lakeshore before he died."

"It's a gorgeous view, but I like the one from your house just as much." She turned around and came back to where he was seated, sat down beside him but kept as much distance between them as the swing allowed. "All right, we're here where no one is going to interrupt us. What's going on?"

He took a deep breath of her, all warmth and spice and woman. She was wearing a camisole top in a soft apple green that beckoned him to reach out and explore the soft curves beneath. He forced his gaze upward and found her regarding him with narrowed eyes. "What are Trey and Adam up to?" she repeated, not giving an inch.

He had warned his boss he wouldn't keep any secrets from her, not if she agreed to stay with him—in whatever capacity he could keep her. "I told Trey this wouldn't work, that you wouldn't fall for that 'good luck charm' malarkey."

"You're right. I didn't fall for it. And I don't want my mother and my sister—" once more her voice broke slightly, and he felt a tiny electric jolt of protectiveness stir inside him "—or Sadie subjected to any more of that media-feeding frenzy like the one outside the hauler in Talladega."

"It isn't going to happen again," he assured her.

"How can you say that? How can you be sure? Those reporters came out of nowhere. And there were others, those people out on the hillside at Phoenix." She rubbed her hand up and down her arm as though she felt chilled. He wanted to reach out and take her in his arms to soothe away the memory of what had happened that afternoon, but she wasn't ready for that, so he kept his hands to himself. Reason was what was wanted here, not emotion.

"It's not usually like that, Cassie. I told you most of the reporters are good people. They don't hound the drivers' families. The Internet guy was just a jerk, that's all. You find them everywhere."

"It's too risky," she repeated stubbornly. "What exactly is Trey trying to keep under wraps? He's trying to deflect attention from something by using us. What is it? He isn't going to all this trouble just to hide meetings with a girl-friend, is he?" Cassie was looking at Ethan now, that arrow-straight assessment that allowed no prevarication, no skirting the issue. She had spent her life watching over others. Her mother, her sister, her country. And now his daughter. She wouldn't back down now.

"What I'm about to tell you is in strictest confidence," he said. "No one outside Trey's immediate family knows anything about it." He reached out to trace the delicate line of her wrist, delicate yes, but in no way frail or weak. She could take whatever fate dished out and give as good as she got. Complete honesty was the only way to go with her. He knew that instinctively. He closed her hands in his.

She didn't pull away from his touch. "You have my word," she said with quiet dignity.

"I knew that without you telling me," he said softly. "Trey has a medical condition. A very serious one. That's the secret we're keeping at Sanford Racing."

"Cancer?"

"No. It's not cancer. It's controllable, but there's a lot of baggage attached to the disease. NASCAR knows all this and has cleared him to drive, but if the media finds out, well, it could get pretty complicated, more than complicated. It could mean the end of his career."

"What's wrong with him?" Cassie asked bluntly.

No more evasions, no more dancing around the truth. He had told Adam and Trey that earlier. He intended to make Cassie Connors his wife, if she would have him, and there weren't going to be any secrets between them. If they didn't want to go along with his decision, then he would resign from the team. Adam had given his okay. Trey had too, eventually. "He has a seizure disorder. In layman's terms Trey has epilepsy. It's not the type that stiffens your joints and makes you lose consciousness. That's a much more serious variation of the disease, as I understand. He has what's called 'absence seizures.' He just drifts off for a few seconds, like daydreaming, is how he explained it to me."

"Those seizures could be just as dangerous as the other kind at 180 miles an hour." Cassie gave her head a tiny shake.

"I agree. But in Trey's case they're completely controlled. He hasn't had one in years. He has a device implanted in his chest. Kind of a pacemaker for his brain, I guess you could call it, that keeps the seizures from happening. The problem is, it's been acting up on him. It needs to be recalibrated and his neurologist is in Mexico."

"Then all the trips to Mexico weren't to meet a woman?"

"The woman in the photographs is his doctor's nurse. She's being seen with him to throw off the reporters, just as he hoped that getting you to go along with the 'good luck charm' bit would switch the focus from Mexico altogether."

"And you agreed?"

"Sort of," Ethan replied. "I said he could try, ask you as a favor. I thought…well, you and Mia are two tough cookies…" He tried out a smile, relaxing a little himself, and must have got it right because her lips twitched slightly. Her expression remained stern, however.

"I think you're right about Mia. She's going to be a formidable woman someday. You hired yourself a winner, Crew Chief."

"She's going to be an asset to the team," he agreed, and meant it.

"But she doesn't want the rest of the team to think she's getting preferential treatment, so Trey's not going to get her to go along, either."

"And you?"

"No way."

"I already told him that."

Cassie wasn't sidetracked for long. She returned to the subject with her next words. "Who else knows about Trey's condition outside of his family?"

"His doctors, of course. And NASCAR. They had to be convinced it was safe for him to race."

"Epilepsy," Cassie murmured, her brow furrowed as she worked through the implications of this revelation. "It explains a lot. I see now why he doesn't want it known. It would cause all kinds of problems for him."

"And for the team. We're having a tough year, Cassie. We lost some key players when Adam didn't renew Toby McPherson's contract and brought in his brother to drive the car. There are a lot of people in the sport who don't think Trey's ready for prime time. They wouldn't be sorry to see him brought down a peg or two."

"It might do more than bring him down a peg or two. It might ruin his career."

Ethan nodded. "And bring Sanford Racing down with him. We've got a bunch of new guys on the team. I'm doing my damnedest, but they just aren't coming together as a cohesive unit the way they should. We need Trey relaxed and focused and driving well to stay in the top thirty-five in points."

"So you're guaranteed a starting position in every race."

"You're catching on fast." He nodded. "None of those things will happen if the reporters keep digging into Trey's private life."

"I understand now." She tapped his chest with her finger. He wanted to reach out and cover her hand with his own, raise it to his lips, kiss her palm, her wrist, but he resisted the almost overpowering urge. Not yet, but soon. Very soon. "You've made your case, but I still can't do it. You're sure you've talked Trey out of trying to make it happen, though, right?"

"Right."

"And his brother, too?"

"Adam is in agreement with me."

"I would be more diplomatic with him," she said with a hint of a smile lighting her eyes. "But with Trey, I'll give him a flat-out no."

"I don't doubt it for a moment." Ethan would never have admitted it, but he'd like to see Cassie take on Trey Sanford, and even Adam, if necessary. It would be a sight to behold.

"If you want Sadie with you at Richmond this weekend, I will come with her and keep her safe and see that she has a good time. But my mother and my sister—and my dog—are not coming along. And I won't go to dinner with Trey or be seen with him. Will you make that clear to your driver, or will I have to do it myself?"

He laughed. He couldn't help himself. "Oh, Cassie, my warrior princess."

She drew her head back looking offended, but there was a smile in her eyes. "Warrior princess? Don't talk nonsense. I'm no warrior princess. I'm—"

"A United States Marine who happens to be a woman. I know and I promise you I'll never forget." He grew serious. This was it. He was going to gamble everything, his happiness and Sadie's, on one more attempt to speak from his heart. "Cassie, about the other night—"

"We should be getting back," she said hurriedly. The amusement faded from her eyes, leaving them the same dark green of the lake water, shadowed and distant. "People will notice we're gone. Sadie will be anxious."

"No, Cassie. We're not putting this off any longer." He

bracketed her face with his hands. "We're going to finish what we started Saturday night. I'm going to ask you to marry me again. And this time for all the right reasons. If you turn me down again, you'd better have a damned good reason why."

CHAPTER SEVENTEEN

A DAMNED GOOD REASON why.

The words were issued in a tone that took Cassie back to her boot-camp days at Parris Island, making her want to salute and say, "Yes, sir!" Ethan didn't stop there. "We're going to talk about us now," he said. "Not Trey's illness or what's wrong with Sanford Racing. We're going to take up where we left off that night in the motor home."

"I told you I'd forget what happened that night. We can just go on being friends. We can just go on being two people who love Sadie and want what's best for her," she said a little desperately.

"No," he said in the same uncompromising tone.

"I don't want a marriage of convenience or whatever it is they call that kind of arrangement these days," she said, reverting to her original attack strategy. She wouldn't give him a chance to say the words. She wouldn't have to hear him ask her to marry him without telling her he loved her, too. No woman should have to suffer through that agony twice. If he did ignore her pleas, she would surely break down into tears again. She could feel the traitorous sting of them lying in wait at the backs of her eyes.

"I don't want one, either," he said patiently. "Weren't

you listening? I'm going to ask you for all the right reasons this time."

Her heart cracked a little and the tears pressed harder. She blinked to hold them back. "I know it would be good for Sadie. I...love her with all my heart, Ethan. I'd be the best stepmother I knew how, but—"

"I know you love Sadie," he said, dipping his head to kiss her on the tip of the nose. "You'll be the best mother you can be. I know that, too. But that's not why I'm asking you to marry me."

"There's no such thing as love at first sight," she said desperately. "I agree with you there."

"Stop talking and listen," he said. "I didn't think I was the kind of man who could fall in love at first sight. I didn't believe in the possibility that it could happen."

"Well, I don't believe, period," she said sharply. She had known him ten or twelve days at least before she fell completely, irrevocably in love with him. "My mother fell in love at first sight with my father. Their marriage was a disaster. He took off and left the three of us to fend for ourselves. We never saw hide nor hair of him again. Not a postcard. Not a phone call. Nothing. Love at first sight doesn't exist. Lust at first sight maybe, but any rational human being can control their sexual reactions if they put their minds to it. Talk themselves out of it—"

"You mean this kind of reaction?" He kept her face between his hands. He leaned closer, his gaze locked to hers until his features swam out of focus and she was forced to shut her eyes. His lips touched hers and then his mouth covered hers, and bells and whistles and warning sirens went off in her head, fireworks blazed in the darkness behind her eyelids. She couldn't think, couldn't speak. Could barely breathe.

"Talk yourself out of that," he whispered, sounding far too pleased with himself.

She sighed. "I don't think I can."

"I sure as hell can't." He leaned his forehead against hers and she felt the tremors that coursed through his body and knew he was just as affected by the kiss as she had been, despite his flip remark.

"Ethan, please. Don't make this difficult for me. I don't want to start an affair that will only end badly and hurt Sadie in the bargain."

"Why do you think an affair would end badly?" he asked.

"Because it would. I'm not good at casual, Ethan. I never have been. I promised myself when my dad left I'd never let my heart get ahead of my brain. I don't want to go through what my mother did when he left us." To her horror a tear slipped past her defenses and slid down her cheek. Because she had done precisely that, let her heart get ahead of her brain.

"You're not your mother," Ethan said, wiping the tear away with the pad of his thumb. "And I'm sure as hell not your dad."

"You can't be sure."

"I am sure. I'm done making deals, Cassie. Deal making is for the NASCAR off-season. I'm dead serious. I don't want a marriage of convenience or some kind of business partnership. I want what I had with Sadie's mother. I want to be in love again."

She closed her eyes a moment, then opened them to face her destiny. "Are you in love with me or just the idea of being in love again?" She had to force the words past the constriction in her throat.

"I am in love with you," he said. "Not the idea of love. Not the memory of a lost love. I knew Sadie's mother five years before I asked her to marry me."

"There, you admitted it yourself. It's too soon. Too early—"

"Hush," he said. "Seventeen days. It's not a long time on the calendar, but it can be a long time for your heart. I love you, Cassie. Today. Tomorrow. For the rest of my life."

"Oh, Ethan, what if you're wrong? What if it doesn't last? I'm afraid." She had never admitted that even to herself. She was afraid to let herself fall in love, head-over-heels in love, because she didn't want her heart broken as Lelah's had been.

"It will last, Cassie. It will last because we'll work at it every day of our lives."

Her heart beat faster. Happiness began to bubble up into her chest. She closed her eyes, listened to the sounds of birds in the trees overhead, a boat motor starting up out on the lake, waves lapping the shore at their feet. But those sounds were on the surface. What she was listening to was deep inside her. She was listening to her heart.

She gathered all her courage and held it close to that glowing warmth, that reckless happiness that was sweeping through her. "I'm pretty sure I'm in love with you, too."

He laughed and pulled her into his arms for another kiss that went a long way toward erasing any shred of doubt. "Will you marry me, Cassie? Will you be my wife? My lover? Sadie's mother and the mother of all the rest of our children?"

Children? She hadn't let herself even dream of that possibility, not for a long time, not since she'd returned from the nightmare of combat. Now it seemed entirely right and natural. She let him wait while she caught her breath. "Yes," she said. "Yes, to all those things. But what—"

He touched his finger to her lips. "We'll take this slow, Cassie. I'll give you time to catch up."

She shook her head. "I'm up to speed," she said, smiling, "but what about everyone else? We can't just drop this on everyone out of the blue. Sadie…"

"Sadie will be thrilled. I think she loves you already." He grew serious. "But you're right. Sadie's grandparents…"

Cassie sobered, too. "They've never met me. We can't do that to them. They need time to get used to not having Sadie with them so much. They'll need time to accept the idea of another woman raising their daughter's child. They need time to get to know me." She leaned back in his arms, feeling overwhelmed once more. "Your family, too. I've never met any of them. And then there's Mom and Mia. I think we're going to have to keep this a secret for a while."

He drew her against his heart. "Slow down," he said. "Stop worrying. As for your mom and Mia, I don't think they'll be as surprised as you may think, but you're right about the others. They need time. And that's one thing we've got—all the time in the world. We'll just take it one day at a time."

She reached up and wrapped her arms around his neck, rubbing her nose against his, smiling as he lowered his head for another kiss. "Oh, no," she said. "If I'm going to be the wife of a NASCAR crew chief, we won't take it one day at a time. We'll take it one race at a time."

* * * * *

For more thrill-a-minute romances set against the exciting backdrop of the NASCAR *world, don't miss*

ONE TRACK MIND
by Bethany Campbell
Available in August.

For a sneak peek, just turn the page!

AT FIFTY-NINE MINUTES to ten, Lori sat tensely in her father's office.

In summer she usually came to work in shorts and a T-shirt, but she hoped she looked like a semi-young professional who had neither overdressed nor underdressed. Feminine, but not too feminine, sensible, tidy and orderly—that's how she hoped to appear.

She wanted to impress the man who'd be the new owner of her father's speedway, so she'd rooted through the pathetic contents of her closet until she'd found a modest white linen sundress with cap sleeves and only a barely visible stain at the hem.

Her old white sandals were polished to a snowy sheen. She wore her hair pulled back and pinned decorously into place with a white barrette. And she'd covered her freckles.

She'd given the staff orders that she didn't want to be interrupted for any reason that morning, although she'd told nobody of her mysterious visitor. For the past thirteen minutes she'd been doing deep-breathing exercises to calm herself.

She didn't want to show her anxiety or burst into tears of relief—or, as she was still tempted to do, fall on her rescuer's neck and embrace him as if he were a hero delivering her from barbarian captors.

So she sat very straight in her chair, her hands on her knees, her eyes closed. *Breathe in to the count of fourteen seconds. Hold breath seven seconds. Exhale smoothly for eight. Breathe in to the count of fourteen seconds—*

A knock shook the door so hard that it rattled on its elderly hinges. Lori's eyes snapped open. The clock on her desk told her that it was exactly ten.

"Come in, please," she said, forgetting to exhale. It made her voice come out too high, almost squeaky.

She leaped to her feet, moved quickly to the door and swung it open to meet her guest. She looked straight at a male chest clad in a slate-gray silk shirt. She raised her eyes to meet those of the visitor. Their gazes locked, hers green, his dark brown.

"Ms. Garland," he said. "I came to make you an offer on your speedway." His face was lazily expressionless, except for a hint of a sardonic quirk at the edge of his mouth. There was a slight scar next to that quirk.

She blinked in disbelief. She now found herself wanting to weep with rage rather than relief. She no longer felt impelled to kiss him for saving her livelihood, but wanted to turn him around forcibly and kick him in the seat of his obviously expensive pants.

He cocked a dark eyebrow. She could tell he enjoyed her dismay, even savored it. "We used to know each other," he almost purred in the low voice she remembered all too well. "You were Lori Simmons then. We were in high school together. I'm—"

"You're Kane Ledger," she supplied. She wished she could

pry up a few tiles from the office floor and burrow down into the earth, deep out of sight. He was the boyfriend from her past that she most regretted and most wanted to forget.

"May I come in?" he asked in a tone that was half silky, half sarcastic.

"Please do," she replied with her finest imitation of calm. She waved him inside, and suddenly the little office looked twice as shabby as before. She gestured for him to sit in the extra chair. It was upholstered in ancient imitation leather, and its seat was patched with an uneven *X* made of duct tape.

Kane nodded and stepped into the room, laying a black leather folder on the edge of her desk. He still had the long, lean body he'd had as a teenager and that air of being at once both casual and dangerous.

And, to her discomfort, she saw that he still had that same sell-me-your-soul grin. It made her pulse quicken and her nerve ends tingle. His presence galvanized the little room like a gathering lightning charge.

She sat, and gestured for him to do likewise. *Get control of yourself,* she scolded. *What happened was half a lifetime ago. We're adults now. We were hardly more than children then.*

But there was no longer any vestige of boyishness in him. His shoulders had broadened, and his face no longer bore the haunted, too-thin look of someone who knew what it was like to go hungry. He'd finally grown into those beautifully carved cheekbones, and they no longer cast hollow shadows on his face.

As a teenager, he'd already had frown lines etched between his brows. But as poor and underprivileged as he'd been, he'd been handsome. Oh, how handsome. And he was more so now.

He looked tan and fit, and the frown lines were balanced by the laugh lines at the outer edges of his eyes. His hair was no longer ill cut and tousled. He still wore it a bit long, but it was expertly barbered and still as dark as night, no hint of early graying.

Long ago there had often been something troubled in his expression, an almost constant wariness. That air was gone now; he seemed confident. Perhaps too confident and too hard-edged.

He crossed his leg over his knee and studied her. "You haven't changed."

Liar, she thought, with a twinge of deep sadness. She was twenty-one years older, her marriage had failed, she was no longer the town's princess and although she hated to admit it, he frightened her more than a little.

All those years ago she'd encouraged him to want her. She'd claimed to love him, but in the end she'd treated him abominably. He'd quit high school and disappeared from town, and for more than a decade she'd worried that she'd ruined his life.

Then word had come that, in spite of the odds, he'd made a success of himself. He'd become a lawyer, then a sports agent, a powerful one. She'd been sincerely glad for him, but to tell the truth, she'd felt more glad for herself—she wouldn't have to carry so much shame over what she'd done. But she still felt guilty, and knew she should.

Something in his face told her that he knew it, too. She'd made him suffer. Was that why he'd come back?

Had he heard about her distress and decided that it was payback time?

She didn't like the cold gleam in his eye or the self-satisfied twist of his mouth.